The Memory Keeper

The Memory Keeper

A work of literary fiction in diary form

S. Nadja Zajdman

Bridge House

British Library Cataloguing in Publication Data
A Record of this Publication is available from the British
Library

ISBN 978-1-914199-18-9

This edition published 2022 by Bridge House Publishing
Manchester, England

This book is dedicated to the blithe spirit of my father, Abram Zajdman, who was born in Radom, Poland on April 16, 1917, and died suddenly in Montreal, Canada on April 6, 1983.

The reason angels can fly is because they take themselves lightly.

G.K. Chesterton

CONTENTS

COURT JESTER

Montreal, Quebec – The autumn of 1971

My name was Sharon, and I lived in the neighbourhood next to where, my daddy liked to say, he could spit on Hampstead. I hated living in that neighbourhood. We moved there when my parents got onto their financial feet. I spent my childhood in a multi-cultural neighbourhood, but after the Six-Day War my mother's nightmares came back and she felt safer in a ghetto. My daddy detested ghettos. In the neighbourhood my daddy called a Golden Ghetto, I felt suffocated.

I also hated being called Sharon. When you called "Sharon" down the halls of Wagar High, half the school came running. I was called Sharon for my dead grandmother Sarah. Girls whose name began with an "S" were usually named for their dead grandmother Sarah. If you had a dead grandmother Sarah you could be called Shirley or Sheryl or Stella or Sophie or Susan – you could be called most anything – except, of course, "Sarah." So I changed my name. I changed my name to Noela, because I was due to be born at Christmas. But I wasn't born at Christmas. In the year of my birth, in early December, my mother's obstetrician told her he wanted to go on vacation as soon as possible. I've always been accommodating. We all accommodate doctors. My mother's obstetrician gave her a bottle of castor oil, told her to drain its contents and check into hospital in the evening. The wheels being greased, so to speak, I made my entrance in the wee hours of the morning on St. Nicholas Day.

I had a younger brother called Mark. He was called Mark for his dead grandfather Marek, though he'd been named Lucian for his dead grandfather Lucian. Our mum was a maverick who broke with tradition. However, Daddy was cursed with a large and forceful family who ignored what my brother was named, and called him what they liked.

Daddy's older brother also had a son called Mark. In his case, he was even named Mark, too. In an effort to avoid confusion, our older cousin was called Big Mark and my little brother was called Little Mark, but as Little Mark had already grown bigger than Big Mark, you had to be a relative to know who was being talked about.

Big Mark was getting married. He was getting married to Sarah Aida. Sarah Aida was named for her dead grandmother, but since any girl named Sarah-for-her-dead-grandmother couldn't be called Sarah, Sarah Aida amalgamated her monikers, and so became "Serenade." Serenade had a younger brother called Eddie who, as far as anyone knew, was named for Eddie Fisher.

Eddie and I were in the same class. Our lockers stood side by side. Twice a day Eddie and I turned our combination keys in unison. We never spoke; the rules of Peer Pressure forbade it. Eddie was a jock, and subject to the rules. I was fat, and automatically disqualified.

And so, the Marriage Machine was set in motion. The invitations were sent and an official announcement of the nuptials, accompanied by graduation photographs, appeared in the municipal daily and the suburban weekly. Designers were called on the carpet, caterers were chewed up and spit out and seamstresses tiptoed on pins and needles until a co-ordinated menu-and-colour scheme, satisfactory to both mothers-in-law, had been hammered out. The colour code agreed upon was raspberry-fuchsia. It would dominate the bridesmaids' ruffled gowns, the ushers' ruffled shirts, the drapes, the tablecloths, and the food. Three of the bridesmaids were friends of Serenade. The fourth bridesmaid was me.

"Please Mum. I don't want to be a bridesmaid. I don't need to be a bridesmaid. Serenade can have them all from her side. I won't be hurt if they leave me out, really I won't! Please don't make me wear that dress!"

"You're the youngest unmarried female on Big Mark's side. If you don't represent the family, people will talk."

"People will talk anyway."

"But people will think there's something wrong in the family."

"There is something wrong in the family. Everybody knows that. If they don't talk about us, they'll find something else to talk about. Please Mum, I can't wear that dress!"

"The other bridesmaids are wearing the same dress."

"The other bridesmaids don't look the way I do. Please Mum, all Eddie's friends from school will be there. I mean – ruffles, Mum! Ruffles!"

"We'll talk to the dressmaker. We'll see what she can do."

The dressmaker could do little except use more material on me. A riotous design of fuchsia flowers seemed to be growing on my hips and my behind. My waist, or rather the location of my hidden waist, was trapped in lavender, and my breasts, ankles and wrists were rimmed with raspberry ruffles.

Auntie Henia was the only sister-in-law on talking terms with Mum. She sighed. "Maybe we can do something with her hair."

At this suggestion, and because of it, I was sent to a beauty salon. My thick, hip-length hair was too lovely to be left alone. The Romantic Look was in, that season, and my wavy mane was crimped into ringlets. I stared at my reflection as if into a Victorian nightmare. The stylist sprayed the springing coils and pronounced, "You look superb, darling, simply ravishing!" I fingered the hideous ringlets. I was miserable. Why did he do this to me? Does he hate girls that much?

The hair rehearsal over, I snuck out of the salon, pressing a scarf over my head. All I need is a *yarmulke*, I thought, and I could pass for a *Hasid*.

I hurried home and threw myself under the shower. Tears streamed down my cheeks as the rushing water drenched my scalp. They ran and the water ran down them, each commingling with the other.

The wedding day arrived at last. It was a glorious afternoon in mid-autumn. The air sparkled, the sun beamed, and patches of blue flashed through marmalade leaves. No matter. The Marriage Machine wasn't taking chances. Its operators had ordered a plastic tree and artificial grass and had them planted in the synagogue lobby. Dead leaves were raked into garbage bags and sprinkled over a green mat. Two photographers in black tuxedos, purple *yarmulkes*, and raspberry-coloured shirts – with ruffles – positioned Serenade and her bridesmaids around the tree.

The photographers didn't know what to do with me. I was taller than the others, my bulk broke the composition's symmetry, and the silver of my braces attracted the camera's flash. The photographers pushed me, each in opposing directions, back and forth around the tree. Finally, I was parked behind Serenade. "Don't step on my train!" hissed the bride.

"Oops! I'm sorry!" I stepped back.

"Hey you! Why'd ya move? We're trying to fit you into the picture!" I removed my glasses, hoping it would help.

"OK girls. Now smiiile! – ahh – except you, the big one in the back – you understand."

When the photo shoot was over, I crumpled into a corner and watched the procession of florists, caterers and musicians parade past. Vases of violets and pink carnations were laid on lilac-and-fuchsia tablecloths on the round tables spaced throughout the banquet hall. Borscht and pink salmon, red cabbage and radish rosettes, raspberry sherbet and plum compote were wheeled into the synagogue kitchen. Strawberry shortcake, mousse and juice and Jello were lined up on the sweets table flanking a heart-and-cupid centrepiece carved out of cut ice.

A microphone was being tested at the rectangular table of honour. Night Rider and His Knights were climbing onto the bandstand.

"Hey Sharon!" Little Mark sprinted in from god-knows-where. "Sharon!" My brother insisted on calling me by my original given name. It was his form of rebellion. "Have you seen Daddy?"

"No, I haven't seen Daddy."

"Well I need to find him. I don't know how to tie this tie!" Little Mark sprinted out again. A moment later, he darted back.

"Hey Sharon! Auntie Stalin's coming!"

Auntie Stalin was The Big Sister and Queen Bee of the clan. Daddy dubbed her "Auntie Stalin" because she ruled with a dictator's fist.

"You know what I heard Auntie Henia say? She said Auntie Stalin had a special dress made. It's so special, nobody's allowed to see it. You should've heard her going on to Mum. She said it was so fantastic, it was a 'Drop Dead' dress. What's a 'Drop Dead' dress?"

"It sounds like it's supposed to be a dress that's so stunning that when you see it, you could drop dead."

"Yeech. Women are weird. I mean, who cares, anyway?"

Auntie Stalin entered. Solemnly she waddled across the hall, her small and stocky body balancing a constipated face. Her beady eyes focused on Little Mark, and ignored me.

"Marek. Dear Marek. Come to Auntie. Come to me."

My brother obeyed. Didn't everybody? Auntie Stalin stroked Mark's cheek. "Marek. Dear Marek." I stared. Auntie Stalin stared back. She bristled. She turned away.

"Sharon! What's wrong with me?!"

"What do you mean?"

"She likes me! I don't get it! Auntie Stalin doesn't like anybody but she likes me! What's wrong with me?"

Our dad had avoided the proceedings for as long as our mum allowed. Now he came in to check on us.

"*Nu, mein* two little samples? Hasn't this funeral started yet?"

"Daddy! I need you! I don't know how to tie this tie!"

"So? Big deal. You want to look suffocated like everybody else?"

"But Daddy, this is fancy stuff! I have to wear a tie – and I have to wear it tied!"

"*Oysh.* Go to your mother. She likes fancy-schmancy. She likes tying ties."

"Daaaaaaddy!" Little Mark shook his head. Daddy didn't get it. Except that he did. Little Mark skipped out.

"Daddy, where's your tie?"

"I put it in *mein* pocket."

"Aren't you going to wear it?"

"Not until I have to. So, *shepsaleh,* you think we will survive this funeral?"

"Daddy, why do you call wedding funerals?"

"You are right. I shouldn't do that. Weddings are not funerals. At funerals you bury one – at weddings you bury TWO!"

I was used to my daddy's *schticks.* I smiled. "I saw Auntie Stalin's dress."

"You saw The Dress? The famous Dress? *Och mein gott*! And you are still alive?!"

"You won't believe it, Daddy."

"About *mein* sister, I believe anything."

"The pattern and material are exactly like our chairs in the living room. Mum's going to *plutz*. Auntie Stalin is wearing our chairs!"

"You don't say? Well, we should sit on her! Ha! Ha! Ha!" Daddy laughed and laughed. My daddy laughed at everyone and everything, and he did it all the time.

"Noela! We're starting! Get up here!" A ruffled-and-tuxedoed teenaged usher shouted from the top of the stairs. At least he got my name right.

"Well well! Look on this! The circus is coming to town! Hey, you little *momzer*! Where did you get that monkey suit?! Ooooo hooo hoooo!" Daddy jutted out his lip, scratched his sides, and hopped around the hall. The shocked boy vanished.

"Don't worry, *shepsaleh,* it will be over soon. And don't let any junky people bug you. They're air. You don't see them. They're just air." Daddy waved his arm like a wand, and in so doing, dismissed every undesirable. "Thank you, Daddy." Quickly, I kissed him. Then I plodded up the stairs and took my place in line. Auntie Henia's son-in-law sidled up to me.

"Hey Noela. Haven't seen you for a while. You're lookin' good, ya know."

"Saulie, please. Don't make fun of me."

"Naaaw, hey! I mean it. You're growin' up, know what I mean?"

"Saaaaulie." I blushed the colour of my dress.

"Naaaaw, really. I like Big Mamas. Something to hang on to. These scarecrows here, they're so skinny, you could cut yourself on them." Saulie smirked.

"Ahhh, is Sophie around?"

"She's with the kids. Susie's one of the flower girls.

14

They've stuck so many petticoats on her, she looks like a potted plant. Waddaya say? Ya gonna be sittin' with us at supper, sweetheart?"

My cousin's husband grinned lasciviously. I was mesmerized by the movements of his tongue. A narrow pink sliver, it darted in and out of his mouth like a reptile's tongue.

"Hey Sharon!" Little Mark sprinted in from god-knows-where. I snapped out of my trance. "What is it, Mark?"

"I figured out why Auntie Stalin likes me but she doesn't like you. It's because you're 'Mum's Daughter' and I'm 'Daddy's Son'!" Little Mark pronounced, proud of his powers of deduction.

"Mark?"

"Yeah Sharon?"

"Get lost." I was ticking like a bomb about to explode. That much, Mark understood.

"OK." Mercifully, for both our sakes, my little brother sprinted off and out of my sight.

The wedding march started. The procession paced in time, as we had been drilled to do. I somnambulated down the aisle. When I reached my designated position, my right ankle began to itch. Surreptitiously I scratched it with my left foot under the folds of my ruffled gown. I gazed at the canopy, at the backs of my cousin and his bride. I felt the collective breath of the congregation, witness to this ritual, as they had been throughout the course of time. I looked at my cousins and classmates, frozen as though in a portrait of still life. I listened to the rabbi's sepulchral tones echoing through the temple, and sensed the eternal question being inwardly asked. Did they, or didn't they? Saulie was standing, protective and paternal, behind his little girl. Did they, or didn't they? I vowed then and there that I wouldn't be a virgin when I married. No one was going to wonder about me.

15

Big Mark smashed the glass placed under his foot, and the stillness was shattered. The mothers-in-law cried, and the fathers-in-law sighed. The younger children snickered, and the older ones cheered.

Supper was being served. The guests were finding their seats. Place cards had been set on the tables. Trying to find my place, I discovered that I was relegated to the side with Auntie Stalin's grandchildren and their nanny. I took my seat beside them, dutifully keeping the place relatives assigned to me.

"Where is *mein* daughter?" I heard Daddy's shout of concern. "Why is she not sitting with her cousins?" Daddy quickly found me. "*Shepsaleh!* Vot are you doing here?"

"Looks like they put me in the sandbox, Daddy."

"VOT?!" Daddy glared at Auntie Stalin, who was safely entrenched behind the table of honour. "Noela! Get up. Get out from there. *Psiakrew cholera!*" Daddy tossed his head like a woman showing off a thick mane of hair. "I'm insulted!"

You fight me, you fight my gang, and Daddy was my gang. He pulled me behind him and bowed before the table of honour.

"*Diekuje, Pani Stalinka!* And a *bon appetite* to you!"

He turned on his heel, snapped his fingers, and summoned a waiter. "*Garçon!* I want another table! Two chairs, and a table."

The waiter stood dumbfounded.

"Step on it, step on it! You got no more tables in this tavern? I want a private table and you can put it near the kitchen. I like food, I'll get it faster!"

The startled waiter stared at Daddy, and then looked to Auntie Stalin for help. There was no help coming. The hapless waiter was trapped.

"I don't want we should sit in the middle." Daddy pressed on. "Put the table against the wall. In the back, in the corner, where I can watch everybody making fools from themselves!"

The dumbfounded waiter stood paralysed.

"Come on come on come on!" Daddy didn't have all day. "I haven't got all day. MOOOOVE!"

Daddy's command gave new meaning to the term "jumpstart." The waiter jumped. A table and two chairs materialized.

"Noela, sit down." Daddy ordered. "Sit down with your back to the wall. Always remember and never forget; first rule in a fight, find yourself a wall. This way, nobody can attack you from the behind!"

Auntie Stalin fumed, yet she knew it was dangerous interfering with Daddy. Auntie Stalin and Daddy often locked horns, like bulls. Though they didn't realize it and would never have admitted it, even if they did, Auntie Stalin and Daddy were much alike, except that Daddy played fair, and Auntie Stalin didn't.

My older cousins were seated together. "Uh oh! Uncle Abram's up to something. There's gonna be fireworks! Come on guys, let's go where the action is!" My cousins converged upon us. "Uncle Abram, can we sit with you?"

"No!" Daddy dismissed them instantly, and irrevocably. "Go back from where you came." It was a phrase Daddy had heard too often, under different and dire circumstances.

"Vot's the matter with you?" My cousins weren't taking Daddy seriously. They didn't yet recognize that he was in dead earnest. "Can't you see that this is the head-table? That other table with the idiots behind it – that's a imitation head-table. Where I sit is the head-table, and only the best

17

people can sit on this table, which means nobody except me and *mein* daughter. Beat it!" My cousins backed off, *pronto.*

Mum was trapped with Little Mark at a round table occupied by outraged relatives. Little Mark chomped away at the food set before him, clueless, as usual. Mum knew that no matter what kind of stunt Daddy pulled, she would be blamed for it. Yet she wiped her hand over her mouth, hoping to hide her smile, anyway.

Once we were ensconced at Daddy's self-designated table of honour, he ordered dinner for us as if we were in the most elegant restaurant, and he and I the only couple in the room. Then the moment Daddy wished would never come, came. Big Mark's father rose to make a speech. As president of their *landsmanschaft,* he made a speech at every *landsman's simcha.* It was common knowledge that each time Big Mark's father rose to make a speech, Daddy rose to leave. Big Mark's father approached the microphone. All eyes were on my daddy.

Big Mark's father opened his mouth. Daddy rose from his seat.

"Hey, Abram! Just because he's your brother, you think you can take off while we have to sit here and take it?"

Daddy spun around. "Listen Yacov, I have to go to the bathroom, because if I listen to that laughing-stock I'm going to make in *mein* pants. I have to go to the bathroom, and *mein* daughter has to go to the bathroom. We BOAT have to go to the bathroom, and when ya gotta go, ya gotta go!" Daddy bolted. I followed, wiping my hand over my mouth, hoping to hide my smile.

"*Fuiu*! Let's get out of this tavern. I need air!" Daddy ripped off his tie and stuffed it into his pocket. We walked out of the synagogue and into the crisp evening breeze, strolling arm-in-arm along the tree-lined avenue.

"In nineteen-hundred forty-four I carried that boy on the

steppes from Siberia. They said he wouldn't live, but I didn't believe them. I carried that little baby twenty kilometres to the nearest hospital. He needed a transfusion, and I was the only one healthy enough to give it to him." Daddy recalled Big Mark's inauspicious beginnings in the autumn of 1944. "I gave him *mein* blood!" Daddy almost spit. "And for vot! For vot?!" Daddy answered his own question. "So that twenty-seven years later I should live to see him getting married – in a pink shirt – with ruffles! – to a girl who wipes the floor with her dress?!" The man was incredulous.

"It's called a train, Daddy."

"Vot you talking?" Daddy spoke my language, but no one seemed to be speaking his. "I know vot is a train! A train – goes to Toronto! It doesn't wipe the floor! Huh! One day she will wipe the floor with that joker she just married."

Daddy was on a roll. One didn't dare interfere, nor interrupt Daddy when he was on a roll. "She should wipe the floor with him!" Daddy lined up his pins, picked up his bowling ball, and took aim. "He's the BROOM!" His punchline delivered, Daddy felt better, but not for long. "*Psiakrew*! I should've left him on the steppes! Big Mark has *mein* blood and I want it back!" Daddy then expressed his greatest regret. "Vot for I came to this country? *Ach poo!*" Now Daddy really did spit. "I should've gone to a *kibbutz!*"

"Daddy." I was beginning to wonder. "Are you disappointed in me too?"

"Vot?!" If Daddy was incredulous before, he was astounded, now. "*Och mein shepsaleh,* with your smart dark eyes and such a clever *punim*? Disappointed in you? NEVER!" Daddy laid to rest all doubts for all time.

"But I'm not slim and pretty like everybody else."

"Listen *lemeleh.*" Daddy's tone softened. You was a beautiful baby, and you was a beautiful little girl. Now you are going through an adjusting time. You will be beautiful again." Daddy asserted.

If my daddy said so, then it must be so. Still, in this case, I wasn't sure.

"Other people don't see me that way."

"Other people are stupid!" Daddy was on the verge of spitting again.

"Daddy, would you rather I be fat and smart, or slim and stupid?"

Daddy was amazed that I would raise such a question. For him, it was a no-brainer. "Fat and smart, of course. Because if you are smart, you will be enough smart to lose weight, and then you will be slim and smart, but the other people will still be stupid."

"Ahhh Daddy." I leaned my head on his shoulder.

"Look, *shepsaleh.* Give a look on the moon. Tonight the moon is full, but it is not always full." Daddy shifted into bedtime story mode. When I was a toddler Daddy put me to sleep inventing bedtime stories. Sometimes he put himself to sleep inventing these stories, and I would climb out of my bed, cover my daddy with my blanket, then toddle off in search of my mummy and warn her not to make noise. Now, on this fresh fall evening Daddy narrated, or invented, "Did you know that once upon the time the moon, he went to his tailor because he wanted the tailor should make for him a new suit from clothes? Well, the tailor, he took the measurements from the moon, and he told him that he should come back on the next week. So the moon, he came back on the second week, and in the meantime, he put on weight. The tailor, he said, 'I can't make for you a new suit from clothes because you are heavier then the last week. Go home and we try again next week.' So the moon he went away, and then came back on the third week, and he was even heavier then he was on the week before. Now the tailor, he was starting to get really frustrated, so he said to his client, 'Now listen Mr. Moon, how do you expect I should make for you a new suit from clothes if you are putting on weight all the time?! Now go home again and I give you one more week, and that's final!' So the moon went away again and when he came back on the fourth week he had taken off all his weight, and then he was just as slim as he was when he went to see the tailor on the first time. Well, by now, the tailor, he was *sahitst-samitst*. He could never fit the moon because the moon was always changing, and so it came out that the moon could never have a new suit from clothes." End of story.

My daddy and I wandered along the darkened shadows of the avenue a little while longer. "If we don't go back," Daddy sighed, "your mother will catch the hell, and if your mother will catch the hell…" Daddy was grimly conscious of the consequences, "…then I will catch the hell. I am spending so much time with *mein* moon that your mother, she will say, 'How's about you should spend time with your 'sun' too?' " So, reluctantly, we returned to the temple.

Dinner was over. The band was playing. I began to tap my feet, to snap my fingers, to twitch. Mum noticed. Silently, she signalled Daddy. Daddy had noticed, too. He winked at Mum. He nodded. "Come on *shepsaleh,* let's dance!"

"Oh Daddy, you can't dance. Everything you do is either a fast *hora* or a slow *hora*."

"Well, so teach me!"

"OK But the first thing you have to learn is that there's no touching."

"Vot? No touching? Then where's the fun?"

"Daaaaddy! You have to feeeeeel the music. You just have to feel it, that's all!"

"HOK KAY! So I feel it!" Daddy thrust out an arm and

kicked out a foot. *"Och,* I am feeling it!" My daddy valiantly attempted to get into the groove, though funk was neither Daddy's bag, his thing, his inclination, nor his groove.

"I am getting hot! I am getting hotter! I am getting so hot that I am catching the fever! It's Saturday night," Daddy added impishly, "So I am catching the Saturday Night Fever!"

Daddy overestimated his hotness, if not his coolness. He posed no threat to John Travolta (and the disco king was no match for my daddy). "Daddy." I tried to dampen his enthusiasm, as though I could. "You look like you're doing karate."

"I do? You mean like Elvis?" Daddy was like a buoy on the water, constantly bobbing to its surface, no matter what nor who tried to push him down. *"Och* boy! I am dancing like Elvis!" Daddy had entered The Zone. "Hey *Stalinka,* look on me!" Daddy jutted a hip at his disgusted sister. "I am 'Elvis the Pelvis'!" Flailing his hands, he smashed imaginary bricks in the air. "Karate! Karate! Chop! Chop! Chop!" Daddy not only entered The Zone; he entered the zeitgeist.

"Abram! At your age? You'll get a heart attack!"

"Yacov, you *alte koker*! Get outta here!"

"Oh Daddy! That's not how you do it!" To keep my daddy from embarrassing himself, I had no choice but to show him how to dance the way my generation danced. "You do it like this!" I whipped off my glasses. "Here. Hold these for me."

My amused dad held my glasses, while I launched into a demonstration. The Godfather of Soul had nothing on me. "I feeeeel good!" Night Rider shouted out, as a wailing saxophone nodded in assent. In response, I shimmied and shook. I sailed across the floor feeling weightless and free. "We knew that we would now." Night Rider's Knights bopped in unison. "I feeeel good!" Night Rider reiterated, as I thrust a fuchsia-flowered hip at my delighted daddy. (He knew that I would now.) "So good!" Night Rider was becoming redundant. "So good!" I swivelled my hot pink hips and aimed both index fingers, like popguns, at my beaming daddy. "I got YOU!"

The music stopped on a dime, and so did I. Parents applauded. Children roared. "Wayda go Noela, wayda go!"

I grew disoriented. Having discarded my glasses, the crowd became an innocuous blur. Now I sensed them closing in on me. The music started up again. I felt empowered and joyful in rhythmic movement. I performed in the centre of an admiring circle. Then I was asked to dance. By everyone. Even Serenade's jock brother Eddie.

"Boy, Little Mark, your sister's really talented. Is there anything you can do?" My brother was leaning belligerently against the counter of the bar, tippling at a bottle of Seven-Up.

"Me? Huh!" Little Mark sniffed. "I don't have to." He was unsettled by the attention I was getting. He wasn't used to it. Neither was I. Little Mark got his bearings before I did.

"All I gotta do," my little brother blustered, "is stand here and look good!"

Daddy strutted over to Mum. "Hullo Beautiful. Wanna dance?"

Mum jabbed Daddy a left to the lower ribs. "Abram! *Usokuj sie!* Abram! Behave yourself!"

"Abram, that's a helluva live wire you got there. A real apple from the old block!"

"*Oysh,* Yacov. Tell me, baby, about it. Now THAT one has *mein* blood!" Daddy wrapped his arms around Mum and hugged her hard.

"Abram! Your sister is looking!" Mum blushed the colours of my dress.

"So? Let her look! Let them all look!" Then he signalled Night Rider. "*Maestro!*" Daddy hailed the leader of the band. The band members perked up. "*Maestro!* Am I allowed to make a request?"

Night Rider nodded. "Certainly sir, you're allowed to make a request."

"Hok kay. So I request you should play the first thing that you played when you got here. You know, when only the bride and the broom was dancing? Do you remember it?"

"I hope so."

"Well I hope so too!"

"It's called *The Wedding Waltz*"

"Votever. Me and *mein* wife, we never got no wedding – all we got was supper in *mein* sister's house."

Behind the imitation head-table, Auntie Stalin sniffed.

"So I request" – Daddy registered his sister's sniff, but chose to ignore it – "that what you played before, you should play now. I want to dance with *mein* lovely bride."

The congregation laughed. Auntie Stalin seethed. Mum made a break for the door but Daddy was faster, and dragged her back. "Just like the way we got married, eh, *mein* former girlfriend? You made me chase you until you caught me!"

"I did not!"

"Oh yes you did." Daddy leered at Mum, as if he were Groucho Marx. "I knew you really wanted me – you was just saving your face!"

Daddy led Mum onto the dance floor. Some sentimental electrician dimmed the lights, and *The Wedding Waltz* was played once more.

I cuddled up to Little Mark as our parents glided together across the hall. I kissed him. He punched me. "Mark?! What did you do that for?!"

"I dunno." Little Mark pursed his lips. He looked up from under lowered lashes, and suddenly offered, "Wanna sip of my Seven-Up?"

"I don't drink Seven-Up – but if you really mean it," Magnanimously, I allowed Little Mark to make amends. "I'll let you get me a Perrier."

AN ANGEL AT OUR TABLE

Montreal Quebec – Early Spring, The 1960s

Auntie Stalin was a sour woman. The only person she showed affection for was my little brother Mark. Perhaps it was a form of displacement. I suspect it went against Auntie's principles to demonstrate her true feelings for her own little brother. As a boy, Daddy was a prankster. As a man, he donned the cap of the court jester. Yet each Passover it was Daddy who led the Seder service, even though it was held in his brother-in-law's house.

Although he was raised to become a rabbi, Daddy turned to socialist rebellion. He could recite the Haggadah backwards, forwards, with full expression, and at any speed he chose. One year, Auntie Stalin informed my male cousins that they could be excused from the table to watch the hockey play-offs if the service ended before the game did. Hockey play-off games go on forever –but the Seder service goes on longer. Auntie's mistake was to make this promise within earshot of Daddy.

At first, the shift in rhythm was imperceptible. Daddy began chanting more quickly than usual, and the uncles dutifully picked up the pace. Incrementally, his chanting grew faster and louder and faster still, until he was hurtling through the *Haggadah* at the tongue-twisting pace of a Danny Kaye patter song. Daddy kept his head down, his face straight, and his eyes fixed firmly on the Hebrew text before him. The uncles were forced to follow as best they could. Auntie Stalin fumed in helpless fury. The boys beamed. Before the evening ended, they got to see the last part of the hockey play-off game.

It is the role of the youngest child to open the door for Elijah, prophet, angel, and protector of children, so he can enter the household and drink from the goblet of wine that has been prepared for him. By rights that task should've been performed by my little brother, but when the moment comes for the participants to dip their pinkies into their wineglasses ten times to symbolize the ten plagues which have befallen Egypt – and it comes before the entrance of the angel – Mark would cuddle up to Mum and merrily dip his pinkie into her wineglass along with her. Whereas Mum would then wipe the residue onto a napkin, like the rest of the grown-ups, Mark would remove the wine from his finger by licking it off. Ten drops of *Manieschewitz* was enough to knock him out, and he'd spend the rest of a very long evening curled up on Mum's lap, his pudgy palms clasped as if in prayer and pressed against a cheek, his *yarmulke* askew on his flaxen crew cut, a beatific beam on his cherubic face. Thus, the role of gatekeeper fell to me.

"You mean to tell me that he comes to our house and to everybody else's house all at the same time?" I'd query my dad, when instructed to stand watch.

"Well he's an angel; he can do that. Except in Israel. In Israel he gets there seven hours later, because of the time change."

As my aunts and uncles and older cousins remained at the long dining table continuing the recitation, I was told when to open the door. I was informed when Elijah finished his drink, and then I was directed to close the front door to my aunt's duplex because Elijah had just made his exit.

"But I can't see the angel!"

"Look harder," urged my father. I squinted.

Daddy smiled his warm, gentle smile. "*Shepsaleh*, you have to look with different eyes."

My big cousins sniggered. The entire tribe insisted they could see Elijah clearly. It occurred to me that, surely, if I

27

joined my relatives at the table, I'd be able to see the angel too.

"Why can't I just come back to the table and watch the angel drink the wine? Why can't he let himself out?"

"It's not polite to let a guest leave alone. With an angel, you have to be a gentleman."

I had no answer. Yet.

By the time I was eight, I was fed up with this game. "I don't care if I'm a gentleman or not! After I open the door I'm coming back to the table! I want to see him drink!" I was adamant. Daddy quickly improvised.

"OK. You can come to the table and you will see the angel drink." (Mark still couldn't hold his liquor.) When cued, I opened the door for Elijah, as I did every year. I marched back to my aunt's dining room table. Maybe I walked behind Elijah, maybe alongside him. If I bumped into the angel, I didn't notice.

I stood among the adults in front of my aunt's long dining room table which held a large, ornate silver drinking vessel filled to the brim with a deep burgundy-coloured wine. The moment of truth had arrived.

"OK," Daddy instructed. "Watch. The angel's going to drink."

I held my breath. Daddy slipped his knee under the table and shook it. The silver vessel shimmered under the twinkling crystals of a chandelier. Within the confines of the oval-shaped cup, the dark liquid trembled. I lowered my head and peered.

"It didn't go down!" I scowled. "When you drink there's supposed to be less in the glass! It didn't go down!"

My father's frustration was beginning to match my own. He pursed his lips, and pointed to the goblet.

"Watch again. The angel's going to drink again!" This

time, Daddy kneed the bottom of the table with such force that the wine spilled over the rim and onto the tablecloth – onto my aunt's snow-white tablecloth with the lace trim which she displayed only on special occasions. Auntie stared in horror at the burgundy-hued stain.

I gazed at the goblet in wonder and awe. "Oh!" I gleefully clapped my hands, convinced, at long last. "What a sloppy angel!"

Daddy was satisfied. Auntie sat stewing over the ruin of her finest linen. She glowered at her youngest brother. Daddy met her smouldering glare and softly, sweetly, in English, he reminded her, "You can't get mad from an angel."

BROTHERLY LOVE

Montreal, Quebec – The early winter of 1975

"It's not fair! It's just not fair!" I paced back and forth on the living room's thick carpet.

"I'm sorry, sweetheart," my father offered, lying on the grey velour sofa with a stack of cushions under his knees and *Twenty Letters to a Friend* folded open on his chest, the paperback's spine as bent as his own. "What can I do to make it better?"

"Ach!" I flopped onto one of my mother's petit point upholstered armchairs, the sleeves of my flowing caftan dangling over my narrow wrists. My legs had a visible shape, now. An attractive one. When I crossed them, they comfortably crossed all the way over.

The front door to our large apartment opened, and a mammoth apparition lumbered in and leaned on its beige wooden hockey stick. White plastic skate guards protected the silver blades of its black skates, so big that midgets could paddle in them. Hard plastic shin pads covered its massive calves, and warm woollen socks, red as fresh blood, were pulled up to the middle of its thighs, which were as thick and sturdy as twin oak trees. The bottom of brown vinyl pants, which rode up and around its waist in order to protect the kidneys, met the tops of its socks. The giant's head was hidden by a hard plastic white helmet, his mouth was covered by the double bars of a protruding chin strap, his chest was encased in a scarlet-hued sweater on which his team's logo, COTE ST. LUC CRUSADERS, was printed in bold capital letters, and on the back, the number 4 was emblazoned as an homage to his idol, Jean Beliveau.

"Well look who remembered his address!" Daddy

hailed from his location on the sofa. "Nice to see you, *mein son*! Too bad we have to wait to the spring to remember what you look like."

"Uh," the apparition grunted.

I sulked in the armchair.

"You look upset." Astonishingly, a voice emerged from under the armour of the hard plastic helmet.

"Well I am!" I pouted.

The apparition leaned on his stick. "What's the matter?" He solicitously asked.

"Oh Mark!" I erupted. "There's going to be a BBC production of *The Three Sisters* tonight on that new public station from Vermont, and that amazing actor I saw in New York in June is playing Andrei – I saw him on TV in *QBVII* – he was absolutely stunning – and five days later – not even a week! – when me and Mummy went to New York and I saw that he was playing on Broadway – he came from The National Theatre in London – and Mummy chased him down 45th St. and she got his autograph and I was just dying of mortification and he kissed me! – and now he's going to be on TV tonight and we don't get the channel!"

"It's Anthony Hop Hop Hopkins!" Daddy reinforced the significance of the event.

"Daaaaddy!" My dark, almond-shaped eyes flashed at him. "Really, Daddy!"

"Oh." The apparition acknowledged.

"God Mark! Why do I even bother trying to talk to you! You don't understand anything!" The Phantom of the Forum stood forlornly in the hallway.

"*Nu*, Mr. Jean Beliveau the Second," Daddy chirped, from the sofa. "Hang up your skates. Make yourself from home."

"Hmm." The apparition unlaced his skates, and exited

31

into his bedroom. I flung my long and slender torso back into the armchair.

"Sweetheart, would you like to do your homework again? I can help you."

"Oh, alright." I was a drama student, though when it came to drama, I didn't need much training. I retrieved my heavily pencil-marked script from the top drawer of my bedside table, where I stashed laxatives, returned to the living room, and handed it to Daddy. "Here." I pointed to the scene I wanted to review. "I could use a line drill here."

Daddy adjusted his reading glasses, put aside Stalin's daughter's memoir, held the script with one hand, rested the back of his other hand on his forehead, kicked off the top cushion from the mountain under his knees and, in his Yiddish accent, implored, "Tell me, Toinette, you don't blame me for feeling as I do about him?"

ME (as Toinette, replies): Not at all.

DADDY (as a sweet-young-thing): Is it wrong of me to indulge in these fancies?

ME (as Toinette): I'm not saying that it is.

DADDY (as Angelique, demanding): Would you have me be indifferent to his protestations of love?

ME (as Toinette): Heaven forbid!

DADDY (revelling in the role of ingénue): You do agree with me, don't you, that there was something providential, something like destiny, in the unexpected way we made each other's acquaintance?

ME (as Toinette): Yes.

DADDY (as Angelique, beseechingly): Don't you think that the way he came to *mein* help without knowing me was most chivalrous?

ME (as Toinette): Yes.

DADDY (angelically): He couldn't have behaved more generously, could he?

ME (as Toinette): No.

Daddy (as Angelique, seeking affirmation): And all done so charmingly.

ME (as Toinette): Oh yes.

DADDY (an eager ingénue): Don't you think he's very nice looking, Toinette?

ME (as Toinette): Of course.

DADDY (a starry-eyed ingénue): And that he has a most attractive way with him?

ME (as Toinette): No doubt about it.

(A rapturous) DADDY: And that there is something noble in everything he says and does?

ME (as Toinette): Certainly.

DADDY (wistfully): And no one could talk more lovingly to me?

ME (as Toinette): True.

DADDY (as thwarted naïf. He stumbles over the classical language, yet courageously carries on): And that the way they keep me under restraint and prevent any exchange of the tender affection that mutually inspires us is too annoying for anything?

ME (as Toinette): Quite right.

Daddy (as Angelique, mooning): "But, *mein* dear Toinette, do you think he loves me as much as he says he does?" Daddy extended the script away from his face, shook his head and peered at me over his reading glasses, dropping out of one character and into another.

"You got a hard part, here."

For the first time, I smiled.

The jangle of keys outside the door of the entrance alerted us to the arrival of the matriarch. "HELL LOW! I'M HOOOME!" Mum trumpeted her entrance like the musicians in Elizabethan costume in front of the Festival Theatre at Stratford. "Abram! What on earth are you doing!" Mum accosted Daddy, who was splayed across the sofa, languishing like *La Dame aux Camellias.*

"Vot does it look like!" Daddy shot back. "I am rehearSALing!"

"Oysh." Mum's slanted slate-blue eyes rolled in their sockets. "Help me with these bags, FLATso." Mum pushed her purchases on me. "You should see what I got for you!" Mum was having a field day outfitting me. For the first time, she could. I still refused to choose my own clothes because when I was fat, shopping expeditions always ended in tears.

"I found this gorgeous gown on sale at the new shopping centre across the street – imagine, all those stores under one roof – the only other place you can go from store to store without getting cold is Place Ville Marie! Anyway, it has draped shoulders, a cinched waist, and it's a size 10. With your height and your figure, you'll look like a goddess!"

"Size 10! That's ridiculous, Mummy."

"You have a distorted image of yourself, darling. The saleslady said that if you don't like it, I can bring it back."

"So, Lady Boss," Daddy inquired, eyeing the bags. "How much money did you save today?" Mum and Daddy were partners in life and in business. Mum did the buying and Daddy did the selling.

"You know it's against my religion to buy anything at full price." Mum came as close to answering as she ever would. "I hate to sell, but I love to buy! What I found to show off your figure, darling. Go ahead. Try it on."

I had been a chubby child, and in high school I was heavy. Mum struggled with her weight, and with my weight, for what seemed like all my life. "Later." I ducked. I would never try on clothes except in complete privacy. I explored my mother's closet when my parents were at work and Mark was out playing hockey. I kept no mirrors in my room. I borrowed the outfits I fancied, unaware that Mum had planted them in her closet especially for me.

"Where's your brother?"

"In his room."

Mum knocked on Mark's bedroom door. Mark and I had been taught to knock on closed doors. Mum set the example. "Hi Mark!"

"Ummm," Mark acknowledged. He had changed into jeans and a pullover sweater. Without his protective gear, he looked like an intelligent Elvis Presley. At the moment, he was on the phone.

"He's on the phone!" Mum announced, to the world and to the family.

"He can talk?" Daddy cracked.

"When he wants to!" Mum defended. "Go on, sweetheart." My mother foisted the bag on me. "Give me pleasure. Try on the dress."

When I wore make-up and managed to keep in my contact lenses, my classmates in theatre school compared me to Mary Tyler Moore. My mother saw me as Jennifer Jones. I saw myself as perpetrating an illusion. I felt like a fraud.

My room was at the back of the apartment. I retreated towards it. On the outside of its door hung large, dark wooden comedy and tragedy masks Mum had brought back from a business trip to the Philippines. These masks would leave home with me and, in later years, hung anywhere I came to live. To guests, I would introduce them as "my parents."

The intercom rang. "Awwww! Shut that thing up!" Daddy howled. He couldn't cope with technology. Daddy would die before computers came to dominate.

Mark emerged from his lair and went to answer the

buzzer. The daughter of Comedy and Tragedy dropped the bag.

"Hey Buddy!" The door blew open, and Laurie lassoed Mark with a television cable. Mark's sidekick beamed into his best friend's impassive face. "Your wish is my command!" Laurie was the Lewis to Mark's Martin; the Costello to his buddy's Bud Abbott. He was long and lanky, had a mop of ginger-coloured curls, startled sky-blue eyes, a hiccupy laugh, a visage seemingly made of rubber, and made one think that David Kaminsky must've looked like Laurie before becoming Danny Kaye.

"Yeah yeah. I love you too. Now how do we do this?"

"My dad showed me. On the balcony." Laurie's dad was a TV repairman. The two boys hoisted the cables, and Mark slid open the sliding balcony doors. It was the darkest time of year. Light snowflakes, delicate as doilies, drifted onto the balcony and melted on its floor.

"*Mishigah!* What are you guys doing!" Mum wailed.

"Noela!" Laurie called, crawling up the outside wall of the 16th-storey apartment. "What time does the show start?"

"What show?" I stared at my brother's best friend as he climbed, like a cat burglar, across the wall outside my bedroom window.

"He means the play," Mark translated. He gazed up at his best buddy, who was swinging from a rope he had thrown and attached onto a 17th-storey balcony. "It's not a show, it's a play, you peasant."

"What TIME!" Laurie yelled. His visible breath crystallized in the early winter air.

Daddy was the first to catch on. He remained silent. I got it, too. I did not remain silent. "Ahh, it starts at eight." I stuck my nose outside the balcony door. I felt cold. I always felt cold. Severe dieting had induced anaemia.

"Well," yelled Laurie. "You may not be able to watch

it from the beginning, but you'll get to see it tonight. Mark, hand me the pliers."

Mark assisted as Laurie cut wires and set up a cable strong enough to receive a signal from Vermont. He dropped his feet onto the balcony floor. "Don't you think your sister's overdoing it?" He was uncharacteristically quiet, and concerned. "She looks two-dimensional."

"I know, but she doesn't feel safe."

Laurie sighed. Then he burst through the balcony door. "Done!" He declared. He punched Mark. Mark, bulkier and broader, grabbed Laurie's wrist, twisted his arm, and locked him in a chokehold under the throat. Laurie looked up at Mark, fluttering his long blond lashes.

"Hey, Big Guy. Ya give up?" They giggled at each other. Mark released his hold.

Laurie turned to me. "You're beautiful, you know. It's enough." At that moment, Mark's imposing palm landed on Laurie's back, and he shoved his best buddy out the door. Laurie pranced to the elevator, and Mark pulled on his boots at the entrance.

"Mark!" Mum protested. "It's late. You have school tomorrow. Where are you going?"

"Out," Mark shot back, without glancing up.

"But Mark—!"

"Renia! *Shaaa!*" Daddy intervened, from his post on the sofa. "Mark." Our father's voice softened. "You need money?"

"No Dad. I'm fine."

"You want to take the car?"

"No thanks. Laurie came in his father's car."

"Mark." Daddy declared.

"Yeah Dad." Now Mark looked up.

Daddy nodded, deeply at peace. "Wherever you are going, have a good time."

Mark grinned his crooked Presley grin. "Thanks Dad. I will."

Mark and Laurie were going to Schwartz's delicatessen for smoked meat. If Mark wanted to eat something more substantial than carrot sticks he ate it outside, in order to avoid teasing me. When Mark met a woman who cooked, he would marry her.

"Hey Big Guy! Let's go!" Laurie bellowed, his index finger pressing the button of the elevator door. Mark slung his black vinyl bomber jacket over his shoulder, and joined his best friend.

Daddy returned to reading Stalin's daughter's memoir. Mum unwrapped her parcels. I exited to my room, turned on the television, and slipped back into the reclining chair I had inherited from Daddy. …*And here I am, as you can see. I don't really remember you. I remember only that you were three sisters. Your father has remained engraved in my memory. I have only to shut my eyes to remember him as if he were still alive…* The first act had just begun.

INSULT AND INJURY

Montreal, Quebec – The spring of 1962

I sat at the kitchen table, running my tongue around the loosening tooth in my head. Everyone in my class had already lost their first tooth. Everyone had already had their first tooth replaced by the Tooth Fairy with a quarter under their pillow. Everyone, except for Sheree Nudleman, who held court in the schoolyard, and smoked cigarettes. Sheree swore that her real father was Tony Curtis, and he was coming to get her and would take her to Hollywood as soon as he finished his latest picture. Sheree Nudleman gave no credence to the Tooth Fairy. She insisted the Tooth Fairy was as big a fib as Santa Claus, and told me I was a sucker for believing in grown-up garbage.

As my tongue teased my tooth, I watched Mark's pudgy fingers pat the Jello in his bowl. "Lellow Jello!"

"Mark," Mum reminded my little brother. "Jello is for eating, not for playing. Use the spoon."

"Poom. Poom." Mark picked up his spoon, tapped his dessert, and stared, bug-eyed, as the golden globe wobbled. Mark's Jello was like the sun rising out of the deep sky of its dish. He curled his chubby fingers around the glinting handle, dipped the oval end into the slippery orb, dropped a glob into his open, expectant beak, and cool sunlight slid down his throat. "Ahhhh." A beatific beam lit his full round face. "I like bazert!"

As my tooth twisted, I mused. If there really is a Tooth Fairy, he'd find my tooth no matter where I hid it. Mum and Daddy said the Tooth Fairy would fly in with a quarter. Mum and Daddy wouldn't lie to me.

The terminal tooth dropped onto my tongue. I removed it, like a wad of gum, and stuck it up my right nostril. As soon as I did, I had doubts. Maybe there really isn't a Tooth Fairy, after all – nobody I knew had seen one. And anyway, how would a Tooth Fairy know whose tooth had fallen out, and which pillow to visit? I grew uneasy. Teeth were supposed to sit inside mouths; they weren't meant to ride up noses. I attempted to retrieve my tooth, but it had already disappeared.

Mum was gulping coffee, and Daddy was nursing his nightly glass of tea. Maybe, I reflected, maybe it would be better to tell them.

"Abram! The car!" Mum erupted. She scooped Mark into her arms and herded us onto the street and into the green Chevrolet. Only the front of the car had functioning doors. Deliberately. Mark and I had been taught to climb into the back, and to stay there, so we couldn't fall out.

"But why?" Daddy turned from the steering wheel, to Mum. "Why did the child do such a thing?" Mum's gender, Daddy believed, gave her clairvoyant understanding of his children.

"With her imagination?" My creative imagination was a double-edged sword. "Who knows?!" Daddy sped to the Jewish General Hospital.

"Noely is sick?" Mark was unnerved by the abrupt shift in environment. X-rays were taken of the inside of my nose, but nothing was found.

"Some kids will do anything for attention." The attending physician glared at me. "We have more important things to do." He cast a cursory glance at my frightened parents. "Relax," he growled. "Take her home."

"Noela? Why did you make up such a story?" It wasn't an accusation. Mum knew it wasn't in my gentle nature to intentionally cause trouble.

"I didn't make it up."

"But the doctor says he can't find anything."

"I don't make up stories!" Generally a docile child, I now flared at the doctor. "I'm not a liar! I don't tell lies!"

We shuffled out of the hospital and into the car. Sulkily, I slumped in the back. Mark patted my hand, in sympathy. No one believed me when I told the truth. Not ever.

Several days later, on Sunday, in the afternoon, Mum received a call from the hospital. An alert intern, struck by my staunch defence of personal integrity, re-examined the X-ray, and located the tooth.

I was taken from my family and led into a room that was bare except for a long table and a tray filled with sharp metal instruments. There were two nurses, and two interns. Dr Inhaber had been located on a golf course. The four subordinates were waiting for him to arrive. I was told to take off my shoes and lie on the table. Inhaber entered, scowling. Some stupid kid had spoiled his game. Bypassing anaesthesia, the specialist raised forceps and rammed them up my nostril. I shrieked. Blood spurted out my nose like oil gushing from a well.

"Shut up," Inhaber barked. I gasped in shock. "I said shut up!" Inhaber smacked my rosy, tender cheeks. "I can't work like this." Inhaber turned to his impassive assistants. "Hold her down."

The nurses rushed behind my head. One grabbed hold of my right wrist; the other grabbed my left. One intern pinned down my left ankle; the other bore down on my right. Inhaber, pacified, picked up the forceps again and thrust swiftly, deeply, repeatedly, penetrating high into my head. Fountains of blood spouted through my nose, drenching my dress and the doctor's lab coat. I wailed in agony. Inhaber struck me across the face. Blood flowed from my nares and stained the doctor's hands.

41

"How many times do I have to tell you to belt up, brat!"

My screams turned to sobs as Inhaber slid long metal daggers up my nose and into my head. My fists beat against the nurses, and my feet kicked against the interns. One of the young doctors, his wrists growing tired, sat on my turned-out ankle.

The pools of blood encircling my eyes blinded me. My sobs turned to gulps, and my whelps grew weaker. There was no mercy. I remained conscious.

On hearing my tortured howls, Mark broke away from our parents and charged towards the source of the sound. He stretched up onto his toes, pushing at the doorknob of the examination room. It refused to turn. He pounded on the locked door. He hammered at the block of concrete and launched his stocky body against it like a battering ram.

"Noely! Noely!" Tears splashed his cherubic cheeks. "Dey killing my shister! Dey killing my shister!!!" He pleaded for help to the human traffic in the hospital corridor. He latched onto passing lab coats; he appealed to the humanity of nurses. "Help me! Please help me!"

Our parents were sitting silently on a nearby bench. Mum held onto Daddy. Daddy's hands dangled between his knees. He hung his head like a miserable turtle.

"Do something, Daddy!" Mark screamed, accusatory and confused. "Daddy! Why don't you do something?!"

Daddy's limp hands flew to his anguished face. His hunched back convulsed. Mum held onto Daddy even harder, her slate blue eyes glazing over.

Unable to enlist assistance, Mark hurled himself against the locked door. My cries had subsided to exhausted bleats. Mark pinned his ear against the door. "Noely? Noely?" Was I dead? "Open!" Mark smashed his body against the door. It opened. Dr Inhaber, his lab coat soaked in my blood, stepped out. Mark leapt at him.

"I going to kill you!" He tackled the doctor's thigh and sunk his baby teeth into it.

Inhaber exploded. "Get this little monster off me!" Inhaber hopped on his free leg and tried to kick Mark off his other one, but the tenacious toddler clung to the doctor's trousers, pressed his chest onto the doctor's knee, wept, clawed, grunted, bit and kept biting, as deeply and savagely as his strength allowed.

"I going to kill you," my little brother growled determinedly, between bites and tears. "I going to kill you!"

Startlingly helpless, the specialist pleaded, "For heaven's sake, get him off me!"

Daddy raised his head. His moist chocolate eyes narrowed into dark slits. Mum dug her nails deeply into Daddy's arm. Daddy didn't move. Neither did Mum.

"What's the matter with you people?! Can't you see what he's doing? For crying out loud, I got the damn tooth! Now get this little monster off me!"

I limped out of the examination room. My head was swathed in blood-soaked bandages. Daddy rose to his feet. Slowly, he put his left foot in front of his right foot. Even more slowly, he put his right foot in front of his left one. At the pace of a drugged snail, he approached and pried his son off the doctor.

"It's alright, Mark. Don't cry anymore. Noely is alright."

"I going to kill him! Lemme at him!" Daddy kept a firm grip on Mark as his limbs thrashed and flailed at the empty air. "I GOING TO KIIIIILL YOU!" Mark howled down the hospital corridor. Dr Inhaber escaped into an elevator.

Daddy relaxed his grip, and Mark slid out of his arms.

"Noely?" He flew to me, and flung himself on me. "Oh Noely!" Mark squeezed me to him tighttighttight.

I no longer cried; my skull could not withstand the

pressure of crying. Gently I placed my aching arms on my brother's head, and stroked it. Mum took Mark's hand, Daddy took my hand, and together we left the hospital, glumly trudging to the waiting Chevrolet which had only two functioning doors so that me and my little brother could sit safely in the back seats, without being in danger of falling out.

SOMEONE TO WATCH OVER ME

Montreal, Quebec –The autumn of 1962

In Poland before the war, my mother's sister Ania was a budding fashion designer. In Canada, she owned and operated a dry goods shop.

At Halloween Aunt Ania created wonderfully elaborate and imaginative costumes for her daughter Eva, and for me. In particular, I recall the black-and-orange quilt with matching cap that carved me into a pumpkin. I had the figure for it. However, the remote October I'm reflecting on, I went trick-or-treating as a gypsy. Aunt Ania sewed a rainbow of chiffon scarves onto a belt, which was attached to the area of my anatomy that, we fervently hoped, would one day whittle down to reveal a waist. I wore a real skirt and tights underneath the belt-load of scarves, to keep me warm on this cold autumn evening. I also wore sturdy Oxford shoes, a sober white blouse, and a red wool cardigan. A red sash, with sequins sewn in, was wrapped around my thick dark hair. With my flashing dark eyes and hair, red was my colour. My daddy said so. Eva, who played in the school band, lent me her tambourine. Eva was going trick-or-treating as a prince. The fact that she was a girl was irrelevant. My cousin preferred princely hose to a princess' robe. As a prince, Eva got to wear the mossy green tights she wasn't allowed to wear with her school tunic, and a form-fitting forest-green tunic that her mother draped on her. I inspected my cousin's costume.

"You don't look like a prince."

Eva was taken aback.

"You look like Robin Hood."

"Weeell, Robin Hood could be a prince."

To me, the line of succession was smudged. "How?"

45

Disconcerted, Eva dismissed me. "Oh, you're always asking stupid questions!"

Since I was going trick-or-treating with my older cousin and her best friend Rosie, I warned my father not to tag along. "I'm six years old now. I'm going with the big girls. Don't embarrass me!"

When dusk fell a plump little gypsy, a girl-prince and her slave ventured into the dark suburban streets. Rosie was Eva's slave. Her costume was easy. All she needed were chains. Rosie was also an Elvis fan. On Sundays Rosie would recline on my aunt's plush loveseat playing Eva's Elvis records – not the good songs, but the sappy ones that served as soundtracks to those god-awful movies. While Elvis crooned, Rosie would kiss his image on the record jacket and hug and cuddle its cover. She never seemed to care that she was kissing painted cardboard. Rosie would kiss Elvis' picture ON THE LIPS! She knew I was watching her, and she wasn't even embarrassed.

On this Halloween, the prince and her slave carried sacks ready to be filled with edible treats, but all I had was a penny box for UNICEF. My mother made me do it. There was no point asking anything for myself. Even when I managed to come home with a filled sack, Mum would confiscate my loot and hand it over to the children's hospital.

"If chocolate and candy aren't healthy, then why are you giving it to kids who are sick?!" Like my query on Robin Hood's claim to the throne, I never got an answer to that, either.

Our outing was going well until we turned a corner onto an abandoned street. Our prince had led us there. Eva was the eldest, and she was panic-stricken.

"There's a man following us!" Prince Eva hissed. She

was right. A shadow loomed under a street lamp. We stopped. The Shadow stopped. When we started to walk, The Shadow started to walk. We stopped again. So did The Shadow. Rosie wanted to run, but the chains she'd attached to her ankles, as well as to her wrists, prevented her from doing so. I would never try to run because I knew I couldn't run fast enough. Prince Eva and The Elvis Admirer were whipping themselves into a frenzy. I felt oddly calm. There was something comfortingly familiar about the sound of the tired, flat-footed step falling onto the sidewalk behind us.

"I'm going to see who it is."

"No!" Prince Eva started to cry. She stood paralysed. "Don't turn around!"

"Aw, quit balling." The littlest gypsy scolded her older cousin. "This is dumb!"

I turned to confront The Shadow. It's always best to confront one's shadow. My suspicions were confirmed.

"Daaaaddy!" I shook the tambourine at my taken-for-granted protector. "You promised! You're not supposed to be here! How could you embarrass me?!"

Caught in the light of the lamp, The Shadow hung his head. "I didn't want to!" My father fibbed. Or maybe he didn't. My father fostered independence but father, like daughter, was no match for The Matriarch.

"I'm sorry." Sheepishly, The Shadow apologized. "Mummy made me. You know I can't say no to Mummy!"

MY FIRST AMERICAN

Upstate New York and Montreal, Quebec – The summer of 1967 and the summer of 1999

"Sweetheart. Why didn't you tell us?"

"I forgot. Was I supposed to?"

My parents stared at each other. Once more, Mum prodded. "Were you afraid to tell us?"

"No! Why should I be? I just didn't think about it! What is there to tell?" Mum and Daddy smiled.

It was Visiting Day at Camp Losers, an all girls' camp in upstate New York. My parents placed me there because there was no camp of its kind on the Canadian side of the border. Delicately put, Camp Losers was a camp for overweight girls. Indelicately put, it was a fatty farm.

Early in the season, I was given the option of removing myself from the bunk and moving into an empty bungalow originally intended for use by two head counsellors. Although I was and always would be uncomfortable with communal living, I considered this exclusion a form of veiled punishment. In later years I came to view it as a form of rescue, albeit a lazy one. Camps are meant to socialize children, not segregate them. Fat girls aren't happy campers. Misery may like company, but my bunkmates didn't like me. An eleven-year-old who sits under a tree by the lake reading *The Complete Plays of G. Bernard Shaw* is bound to stick out.

By bunk standards, the bungalow was luxurious. I was offered my choice of roommate. Whom would I like to come live with me? I was drawn to one of the older girls. Lucille Savoie was my polar opposite. She was a fun-loving, rule-breaking extrovert. She had a big smile, a wide nose, and a large appetite. For everything.

Inviting Lucille to room with me caused a scandal at Camp Losers.

"You can't have Lucille! You just can't do that!" my American campmates protested.

"Why not?" I said "eh" for "huh" and pronounced the last letter of the alphabet "Zed." I was baffled.

"Well, you know!"

I didn't know. There was one other girl in camp who came from Lucille's tribe, and she was more virulent than the rest. She was ten years old. She was as wide as she was tall. She waddled up to me on the campgrounds and screamed, "You can't do it! You just can't do it!"

I wasn't the pushover my campmates perceived me to be. Pushed hard enough, I could be as obstinate as my mother. "Why not?" I challenged my attacker. I was beginning to catch on, but continued to feign ignorance. "Tell me why not?" I was going to make this kid spell it out.

"Because!" The wide and dark girl considered me ignorant, and was determined to teach me The American Way. She thrust out her arm and slapped it. "See! You see! Lucille is like me. She's COLORED!"

African Americans had yet to turn black. The descendants of America's original slaves were either Negroes, or they were coloured. I remained stubbornly colour blind, and Lucille moved into the bungalow.

Lucille Savoie came from Washington. Her mother was a schoolteacher, and her father was a high school principal. During The Summer of Love the girl from Washington introduced the girl from Montreal to Motown music, Jive talk, The Ghetto Walk, and the comedy recordings of the guy from *I Spy* (which was a nineteen sixties' television series starring an up-and coming Bill Cosby).

Lucille had brought a record player, along with records, and just before Lights Out she set it up in the space on the floor between our twin beds. She draped a light blanket over the recorder player and, suppressing giggles, we curled up under our own blankets, in anticipation of the nightly visit from a flashlight-wielding counsellor who shone her light through our window and not only expected us to be asleep, but also to remain so. Like black and white angels, we feigned slumber, appearing to comply. When the counsellor was satisfied that we had drifted into DreamLand, like a giant firefly, she floated on. That was when Lucille flung off her blanket, switched on her own flashlight, set a record on the record player, and we'd listen to Bill Cosby's elastic voice bringing to life the vibrant characters of his childhood landscape. Considering the situation our parents placed us in, it was Fat Albert, in particular, who had us pounding our pillows and stifling peals of glee. We dubbed ourselves Fat Albert, and hailed each other in the dining hall howling, "Hey hey hey! Fat Albert! Hey hey hey!"

I was profoundly shy, and in awe of Lucille's confidence. Content to tag after her, I acquiesced to every suggested adventure. After swimming together we'd lie by the lake on a beach towel we shared, bathing in the sun that sparkled on the water and dappled the bottle-green leaves of maple trees. I shared everything with Lucille, so it seemed natural to offer her my suntan lotion, too. She stared at me and burst into maniacal laughter.

Where would I put it? On the back of my feet?!"

"Oh! Oh gee!" Sheepishly, I apologized. "I'm sorry. I forgot."

Even at eleven, I wrote long and descriptive letters. In these letters I told my parents all about camp life and – almost – all about Lucille. Before Visiting Day I damaged my glasses so my parents, armed with a new pair, rode to the rescue from Quebec to the Catskill Mountains. They took Lucille and me out to dinner to the only decent restaurant in the area, which was located in adjacent Ellenville. For Lucille and me, the most outstanding item on the menu was not a main dish, but "a tub of butter and a loaf of bread." The tub and the loaf accompanied anything one might order. What was brought to the table was a deep wooden dish cupping soft yellow butter, and a wooden cutting board holding a large serrated knife and a warm moist brick of dark wheat bread. Released from dietary prison, Lucille and I drooled. On this occasion we maintained our discipline – with Mum The Food Cop within firing range, I had no choice. Also, I was a Miss Goody Two-Shoes. I learned what a Miss Goody Two-Shoes was from Lucille, who took to calling me that when I took to ironing my red hair ribbons on her ironing board. From then on Lucille called me Miss Goody Two-Shoes – when she wasn't calling me Fat Albert. Lucille enjoyed my admiration, and returned it with affectionate teasing.

It was when Mum and Daddy returned us to camp that Mum took me aside. "Sweetheart. In your letters you never mentioned that Lucille is coloured. Why is that?"

"I didn't think about it."

"Sweetheart." Once more, Mum prodded. "Were you afraid to tell us?"

"No! I just didn't think about it! Was I supposed to?" My parents smiled. They had taught by example. In my class at school there was a girl by the name of Shelley White, who wasn't. Her family had moved to Montreal from Halifax. In the schoolyard my classmates taunted her with cries of "Chocolate Fudge! Chocolate Fudge!" I saw that the name-calling made Shelley nervous, and hearing it made me uncomfortable, too. I told my mother what was going on.

"If the kids call Shelley 'Chocolate Fudge'," Mum instructed, "then you call them 'Vanilla Fudge'!"

"Oh!" How simple. "OK." Back in the schoolyard, when my classmates targeted Shelley, I did as my mother told me to do. I really was a Miss Goody Two-Shoes. And the name-calling kids got confused. And Shelley got comfortable.

In our home it was common knowledge that, given the opportunity, Mum would leave Daddy for Harry Belafonte. The caramel-coloured calypso singer who performed in half-open black shirts and hip-hugging black slacks was held as a constant threat in an ever-impending divorce suit. "Great!" Daddy didn't seem unduly concerned. "If you leave me for Harry Belafonte, this would leave me free for Sophia Loren!" Not only was America's first black sex symbol drop-dead gorgeous but also, Mum announced, proud to have discovered common ground with her idol, "He has a daughter named Sharon, too!"

"My name is Noela." Swiftly and firmly, I corrected Mum.

"Oh yes." Mum smiled indulgently. "For a moment, I forgot your name."

"That's OK." Graciously, I reassured her. "But try to remember." I had already decided that I was going to be an actress when I grew up. Besides the fact that there were too many Sharons in my class, if I was going to be an actress, I had to change my name.

Mum felt fiercely protective towards people then referred to as Negroes. The first black person she saw was in pre-war Poland. He was an American musician who'd come on a pilgrimage. Chopin was born in a village several kilometres from her father's hometown. In the 1930s, this black musician journeyed all the way from America to visit the manor house in *Zelazowa Wola.* The urchins of Sochaczew gawked and followed him through the streets. The black musician gave a Chopin concert at the manor house to an audience of curious Polish villagers.

Before the war, one of the many works of literature Mum's father fed her was *Uncle Tom's Cabin*. During the war, Mum was transported to the Third Reich and laboured as a slave. When the war ended she was liberated in the American zone. It was there and then that a 20th century slave, newly freed, saw Uncle Tom's descendants come to life. Black soldiers, as well as white, could pick up a *fraulein* at the drop of a nylon stocking. By 1946, in the rubble of Mannheim, significant numbers of young German women were wheeling carriages containing mulatto babies. Some of them displayed miniature American flags, which waved from the baby carriages. So much for "the master race".

Daddy hadn't any personal experience with black people, but as a Polish Jew emerging from a horrific time and place, he experienced what human beings are capable of doing to each other. Daddy's sense of fair play was as fierce as his *joie de vivre*. Though he dismissed Belafonte as a romantic rival, he was mystified by Sammy Davis Jr.'s conversion to Judaism. He considered the singer *mishigah*. "A *schwartz* with only one eye doesn't have enough problems?" Perplexed, Daddy scratched his head. "On the top of this, he wants to be a Jew?"

On Visiting Day, which extended into a weekend, Lucille's parents arrived on Saturday. My parents were due on Sunday. On Saturday night the Savoies took us to the same restaurant in Ellenville; the one that featured tubs of butter and loaves of bread. Lucille's mother Irma was dark-skinned, petite and slender. Her father Vernon was a husky man, so light-coloured that he could've passed for

Caucasian, if he'd wanted to. At dinner in the restaurant I asked him, "Mr Savoie, if you're a Negro, then how come you got a French name?"

Lucille's father smiled sardonically. His answer was considered, and careful. "Ohhhh Noela, there was a lot of – invasion – in my family." I was confused, but sensitive enough not to press the matter. I didn't understand, for years.

In Lucille's family, her mother was the Food Cop, too. Mrs. Savoie was concerned with her daughter's and her husband's weight. She blamed the problem on her mother-in-law. Lucille and her parents had spent all their summers, until this one, with Grandma Savoie in Louisiana. In succulent detail, Lucille would describe the taste of her grandmother's fried catfish. Mrs. Savoie was trying to inculcate discipline and good nutrition into the family's dietary habits. Hers was a lonely and losing battle.

Lucille was as much her daddy's daughter as I was mine. Once she had her protector by her side, she cut loose. In the Ellenville restaurant, Lucille slathered globs of melting butter onto chunks of hot dark bread. We both ordered lobster. I ate my lobster dry. Lucille soaked tender pink morsels of lobster flesh into the buttery tub. When we were done with the main course, Mr. Savoie offered me more bread.

"No thank you, Mr. Savoie." I answered politely. My table manners were impeccable. "I'm saving my calories for dessert."

Lucille's father moved the bread out of range and struggled to keep a straight face. Lucille didn't struggle. She rolled her eyes in large, exaggerated circles and scoffed, "You really are a Miss Goody Two-Shoes."

My parents turned up the next afternoon. Daddy parked the family car in front of the bungalow alongside a car with a

Washington license plate. Without preliminaries, Mum strode in and greeted Lucille.

"Hi! Where's your mother?"

"I'm in here!"

Upon her arrival, Mrs. Savoie had undertaken a cleaning inspection. The bungalow had failed. Miffed, Mrs. Savoie was cleaning the bathroom. She emerged from the bathroom, wearing rubber gloves.

Neither mother greeted the other. Instead they rolled their eyes, and I shrunk into a corner. Even Lucille seemed slightly shorter.

The two sets of parents instantly clicked. Like the rest of the western world during this Summer of Love, those who weren't flocking to San Francisco with flowers in their hair were heading to Montreal and its wondrous world's fair. The Savoies hadn't secured accommodations in advance. My parents were going home in the evening because they had to get back to work, but the Savoies were staying in upstate New York for another day. Irma asked Mum to book a hotel room for her and Vernon.

My parents were partners in business as well as in life. Their warehouse-cum-office was located downtown, and they generally worked seven days a week. Upon their return to Montreal, Mum went directly to the Queen's Hotel and, with her *Diners' Club* card, reserved a room under the name of Savoie. The French-Canadian desk clerk assumed the room was being reserved for a French couple. When Lucille's parents arrived on Tuesday, Mum met them and accompanied them to the hotel. Aware of what might happen, she planted herself behind the coloured couple like a soldier on guard. When the French-Canadian clerk who had accepted her booking saw the guests she was registering, he glared at her as though she'd played a dirty trick on him. With her steely slate blue eyes, Mum glared back. I knew that glare. The frustrated clerk bowed his head and honoured the booking.

After work, Mum and Daddy had dinner at a friendly family restaurant called *Dora's.* Dora cooked fresh meals every day. When the Savoies finished their daily tour of the Expo site on two astonishing islands off the island of Montreal, they headed back to the city and met my parents at *Dora's.* Daddy introduced Vernon to cheese blintzes, and Mum introduced Irma to potato latkes. Quickly comfortable and cosy, they ate off each other's plates. After dinner the two couples would cross back over the bridge that led to the fair. Strolling through those magical islands at the height of summer, licking at scoops of ice cream cupped in wafer-like cones, the Savoies serenaded my parents with the hit tune of the day; the wistful ballad *People.* When they returned to Washington, Irma sent Mum a recording of the song, which was introduced by and would always belong to a bumpy-nosed, slit-eyed Jewish girl from Brooklyn.[*]

Lucille and I bid a tearful farewell when she developed an ear infection, which prompted her parents to take her home before summer and camp were over. I was left alone in the comfortable bungalow, a situation that appeared to set a template for all the years to come.

My isolation was mitigated by participation in the end-of-summer play. Camp Losers was producing an all fat-female production of *My Fair Lady.* The film adaptation was one of the first grown-up movies I saw. My parents took me to see it. I was learning to look at the small print that comes on before a film starts, and noticed that *My Fair Lady* had grown out of a musical which had grown out of a straight play written by

---

[*] Barbra Streisand

one G. Bernard Shaw. I understood that all those funny, wonderful characters came from the imagination of this one man, and I wanted to know who he was. In a neighbourhood bookshop I discovered two heavy volumes in blood red bindings with the Irish writer's name on it. One of the volumes was titled *Collected Prefaces*, and the other, *Collected Plays*. I had saved up enough money from my allowance to be able to buy one of the volumes. I chose the collected plays because I didn't know what "prefaces" meant.

Holding onto Daddy's hand, I danced out of the movie theatre conversing in a crisp, upper-crust English accent. Daddy was amused and admiring.

"*Oy shepsaleh*, you speak the Qveen's Yingish better than the qveen!" Encouraged by my daddy's reaction, I then mimicked Audrey Hepburn's Cockney drawl. My "aaaoooows" and "gaaarns" were pitch perfect. I had musicians' ears. My sense of rhythm and comic timing were spot on. What I couldn't do was sing, but neither could Rex Harrison, and that hadn't prevented him from creating and reprising a musical role which led from Broadway to an Oscar, so I saw no reason why I couldn't play Henry Higgins, too. Holding auditions in the recreation hall, the teen-age director had other ideas.

"But Noely, you can't play Henry Higgins. You can't sing."

"I know that. I'm not trying for the part of Liza Doolittle – except if you were doing *Pygmalion* I could."

"What?!"

"That's where My Fair Lady comes from!" Oh these Americans. "Look." Patiently, I explained. "I'm trying for the part of Henry Higgins, and Rex Harrison couldn't sing in the movie – he just talked in time to the music. I can do that too – and I can do it with an English accent! You could at least listen to me!"

My shyness was superseded by my desire for the part. I launched into an expressive rendition of *Why Cawnt A Woman Be More Like a Man*. I declaimed the lyrics by heart. My parents had the record of the original Broadway production, so I knew the lyrics to all the songs in the show. I performed the gender-bending tune with a terrifically snooty English accent, yet the teenage director remained unmoved.

"But I'm the only one here who can even do an English accent!" I made one last attempt to persuade the director that I was born to play Shaw's phonetics professor.

"Aww, the only reason you can do an English accent is because you're Canadian! So what! You still can't sing! In my show, the kids who get the singing parts have to be able to sing!"

The theatre is not a democracy. I conceded defeat and shuffled off the stage. "I can't do an English accent because I'm Canadian," I muttered to myself. "I can do an English accent because I can just do it!"

The director of the camp production wasn't totally indifferent to my talent, and proved more receptive than she seemed. Ultimately I was assigned the part of Mrs. Higgins, the professor's mother. Mrs. Higgins is the largest part in the musical that doesn't include a song. I would play mother to a Higgins older than I was.

At first, I sat in on rehearsals even when not called upon to practice. I wanted to see how a play was put together. Bearing witness to the process proved too painful. "Naw repeat efta me: 'Duh rain in Spain stays mainly on duh plain,'" emoted the girl from The Bronx who got the part that I knew, in my bones and in my soul, belonged to me. I threw my hands over my ears and shook my head, the way Daddy did. "Oh no no no no no!" I heaved a heartfelt sigh, the way Mum did. Heavily I exited the shade of the recreation hall and wandered into the shade of the trees. Hugging my volume of collected plays like a precious teddy bear, I sought solace by the lake.

Camp Losers' production of *My Fair Lady* went on with a cast of actresses in varying stages of *avoirdupois*. Those like me, who adhered to the camp diet, approached summer's end in a visibly slimmed-down state. Older girls who managed to smuggle in sweets from Poughkeepsie claimed metabolic imbalances. (One wit hid her stash of chocolates behind the medical scale in the infirmary.)

I scored a personal triumph with my portrayal of Mrs. Higgins. My reading of the line, "Why Henry, I shouldn't have thrown the slippers at you, I should've thrown the fire irons at you!" had my campmates stomping and cheering in the hall. "Boy oh boy! Noely! Who knew?! What a great English accent! You told off Henry Higgins real good!"

"Thank you." With the residue of Shaw's Georgian aristocrat still clinging to me, I remained gracious, yet remote. One of the counsellors looked closely at me. Weight loss accentuated my high cheekbones. Shadow and liner highlighted my suddenly luminous dark eyes. In a long velvet skirt and the high lacy collar of a blouse created by the arts and crafts department, there were outlines of the woman I was going to become. Pensively the counsellor acknowledged, "You should've played a larger role."

My dark eyes flashed, and the Mrs. Higgins in me retorted ironically, "Yes. I should have." This was the one and only time anyone in camp except Lucille paid attention to me. Now I was the centre of attention, and Lucille wasn't there to see it.

When I came home from camp, I wrote to Lucille. In response she sent me a miniature coloured snapshot of herself and autographed it, *Love Always, Lucille S.* Like war buddies, through the autumn and winter we regularly exchanged letters vowing eternal friendship. In the first week of April, an assassin killed the civil rights leader Martin Luther King. In Canada, with my parents I sat in front of our television watching the violent and anguished aftermath of political murder. Mum called Washington and invited Lucille to come to us for the Easter holidays. Lucille declined the invitation because her older brother was coming home on leave from Viet Nam. In the spring of 1968 the Savoies applied for a transfer, and when the school year ended Lucille and her parents moved to Maryland. Lucille was a teenager now. Her letters from Silver Spring came less and less often. Eventually, they stopped.

We grew into young women. Lucille entered the field of education, and I entered the theatre. I realized my dream of working as an actor in England only to discover that as much as I loved the work, I hated the life. Healthy instincts sent me home.

Over the years, particularly at times of crisis in The States, I wondered about Lucille. In 1983, in the first week of April, Mum and I were scheduled to fly to Washington for the second world gathering of Holocaust survivors and their children. Three days before our scheduled departure, Daddy suddenly died. We never made the flight. I deferred dreams of artistic achievement and went to work with my mother.

In the last year of the last millennium I ran an Internet search for the Savoies of Silver Spring. I found a listing for Mrs. Savoie. Irma. In the first week of April, I made the call.

"Noela! Of course I remember you! Lucille will be thrilled! She lives in Washington now. She's a high school principal, like her father before her. She's divorced. Are you married?"

"No. Never married; never divorced."

"Then I suppose you don't have children. Lucille doesn't, either. Too busy with her career. The students have been her children. Oh, wait 'til I tell her about your call! She's in a meeting now, but she'll be home after eight. You can call her then. And how's your mother? I remember her so well."

"She's fine."

"Do you still have your dad?"

"No. He died in 1983."

"I'm so sorry. We lost Vernon in '84. Heart attack. Massive coronary. It took him in an instant."

"That's how my dad went."

"You know Lucille was so attached to her dad. He had high blood pressure. So do I. I can barely walk. I have high pressure, I'm diabetic, and I weigh 200 pounds now." How direct Americans are. Even instantly intimate. I recalled a petite, trim teacher doing a cleaning inspection of the camp bungalow. I couldn't visualize the old and ill woman Mrs. Savoie said she had become.

"Give my love to your mother. She and your dad were so good to us when we came to visit the world's fair. What a time that was. It isn't like that, now."

After eight, I called Lucille. "Noely! My mother told me you've been looking for me. Tell me about yourself! Are you still so sweet? You were so damn sweet!"

I inherited Daddy's pronounced streak of irony. "I used to be sweet. Now I'm bittersweet."

I searched for the Savoies in Silver Spring because I assumed Lucille would be married and living under another name. It turned out that, upon graduation, Lucille returned to Washington and launched her career there. After her

61

divorce she reverted to her maiden name. She was Lucille Savoie of Washington, again.

"What do you look like, Noely? I'm trying to picture you!"

"Ohhh, I'm tall, dark and handsome."

"I remember you with long brown hair which you wore mostly in braids. You tied them with red ribbons. I also remember you as being full of bright ideas, and I remember the way your hands danced when you expressed them." What a lovely way to be remembered.

"My hands are more subdued, now."

Proudly, Lucille proffered, "I've been compared to Oprah." She assumed I would know to whom she was referring, and I did. Americans assumed the world was aware of the talk show hostess and human juggernaut, known by one name, who smashed gender and racial barriers to become one of the most powerful women in America. In this case, they were right.

Now Lucille said what she really meant. "I have the same struggle with weight. I'm still – overweight."

"So am I. Sometimes. It will always be an issue."

Reassured, Lucille invited herself to Montreal. "I can come on the Labour Day weekend, before school starts. Oh, this is so exciting!"

It appeared we were about to come full circle and complete the summer interrupted thirty-two years before. Immediately, I began strategizing. At the time Lucille wanted to visit, Mum would be in Warsaw, serving as a tour guide to busloads of North American teenagers. In the present act of her life, Mum had reinvented herself as a Holocaust educator. I decided to host Lucille in Mum's condo. It was roomier than my apartment. We would have access to Mum's car and to an outdoor swimming pool. I believed Lucille would be more comfortable, there.

Lucille's childhood photograph was still in one of the family albums, but I didn't refer to it. Standing at the arrival gate in Dorval Airport, I was on the lookout for a woman Oprahesque. There seemed to be only white passengers emerging from the Washington flight until a large and pretty chocolate-coloured woman strode through the gate. My heart leapt. I gazed at her and smiled. The woman brushed past me and on to the taxi stand. I continued to wait.

The crowd pouring out of the gate drained to a trickle. I spied a huge black woman dragging a carry-on case. Her kinky black hair had bald spots in it. There were white blotches on the calves visible below her summer shift. She waddled into the hall, and her small round eyes, like chocolate drops, scanned the gathering of people meeting arriving passengers. My heart clutched. "Lucille?" Tentatively I greeted the obese, fatigued woman.

"Noely?"

"Yes."

Lucille's eyes drank in my adult image with a mixture of admiration and dismay. "But." She seemed to insinuate that I had lied to her. "But you're beautiful!" The definition of fat is elastic. At the moment, I was rounder and softer than I preferred to be. What Lucille saw was a strikingly handsome woman in her early forties with haunting dark eyes. At forty-four, Lucille looked an unhealthy sixty.

I was the first to extend my hand. "Welcome to Canada."

I drove Lucille to my mother's condo. En route to a neighbourhood sometimes sneered at as a golden ghetto, we passed a long row of ostentatious houses.

"What would a house cost here?" wondered Lucille.

"I have no idea."

"Why don't you know?" The visitor challenged the local.

"I've never lived in a house."

"Don't you want to?"

"What for? A house is a lot of responsibility. I prefer to be free so I can go outside and play!" I smiled.

"You've still got that enchanting, shy smile." For the moment, Lucille's mind was off real estate. "Except that your teeth are straight, now." At this comment, we both grinned. Then Lucille's attention returned to the view from the car's windows. "I live in a house. My house is big."

"All by yourself?"

"Yes."

"That sounds like a lot of work."

As we rode through the underpass towards Mum's condo the high school principal queried, "Don't you have your own car?"

"Nope."

"Why not?"

"Can't afford it, and wouldn't want to be bothered with the upkeep, even if I could."

"No car," marvelled the American. "Not even one."

In Montreal, the Labour Day weekend of 1999 was shaping up to be the hottest on record. Before leaving for the airport I switched on the central air-conditioning, prepared a light, cold supper, and had breakfast ready too. But for the rest: before Lucille's arrival she insisted that she wanted to shop for her own food.

I unlocked the door to Mum's empty condo. Lucille appeared ill at ease.

"Why don't you get undressed while I set the table. Would you like to take a shower, or perhaps you'd prefer a bath?"

"No, but I sure would like to change." I led my guest to

Mum's large bedroom and then went into the kitchen. In a few moments Lucille joined me, released from her bra and wearing soft slippers and a shapeless housecoat. After supper I introduced Lucille to my family. They were perched on the living room wall. Mum's walls and bureaus were lined with family photographs. Lucille noticed one picture taken close to the time when she first knew me. "That's how I remember you!" The ice was broken.

"Funny, I barely remember myself that way."

At breakfast, I sliced the yogurt herb quick bread I had baked the day before. "This is absolutely delicious!" Lucille scooped up the crumbs. "I want the recipe for this!" After breakfast we went to the neighbourhood shopping mall. The day was going to be a scorcher. "I didn't think it would be so hot in Canada."

"It never used to be," I clarified. "The weather patterns seem to be changing. This afternoon we can go downstairs to the pool. There's a pleasant breeze there."

"I can't sit in the sun." By way of explanation, Lucille raised the hem of her shift, exposing more white blotches on her trunk-like coloured legs. She had a rare skin disease. We would spend the Labour Day weekend in the air-conditioned apartment, the air-conditioned mall, and the air-conditioned car.

As pre-arranged, we went shopping for Lucille's groceries. As the hostess, I insisted on paying for them. In the supermarket she bought a pound of fish fillets. "I love fish."

It's a healthy choice, I thought. Perusing the signs over the supermarket aisles, Lucille gave up trying to find anything by reading them.

"Why are the French signs so large, and why is the English translation in such tiny print?"

"It's a long story." I was rueful. "It's a story covering 200 years of Canadian history."

Lucille cut to the chase. "Where do they keep the butter?"

I led her to the appropriate section. "Over here." I picked up a quarter-pound stick and handed it to her.

"No." Lucille nodded negatively. "Not that one." She leaned over and picked up a sixteen-ounce brick.

"I don't use butter," I intervened. "There'll be too much left over after you leave."

"Oh that's no problem," assured Lucille. "I'll finish it." I hoped I was able to hide my surprise.

Ahead of us in the aisle was a woman wearing a colour-coordinated suit and sandals, who had applied, or had had applied, matching fingernail and toe polish, was a little too loud, wore a little too much make-up and a little too much jewellery, and was blessed with thick, lustrous hair which was a little too stiff with spray.

"Most of them look like that," Lucille scoffed. "Well, they can afford to." She practically spat the words into my face. I was stunned. I knew how Mum had secured the hotel reservation for Lucille's parents during Expo 67, though the Savoies were kept blissfully ignorant of the facts. Where was such a remark coming from? Appalled, I said nothing.

In the evening I prepared a large salad, while Lucille fried her fish. The fillets swam in a pan half-filled with hot, bubbly butter.

"Not like my grandma's catfish," Lucille reminisced. "But it'll do."

Only when the sun went down was it comfortable enough to sit outside on the balcony, but Lucille preferred to watch TV. Mum's set was set to the CBC.

"It's our national station."

66

Lucille didn't bother to conceal her boredom. "Do you get American channels?"

"Who doesn't?" I was an obliging hostess. I switched to CBS.

On Sunday, Lucille saw the sights of Montreal through the windows of an air-conditioned car. I brought her to my neighbourhood, which was a lively multi-cultural district reminiscent of cities in Europe. The former wax museum housed a vegetarian cafeteria.

"This is the neighbourhood hang-out. Here you can choose what you like, take as much or as little as you like, and stay for as long as you like."

I led Lucille to the tables in the back, where a large picture window looked out onto St. Joseph's Oratory.

"This is the postcard view. I can see The Oratory from my bedroom window. On a frosty winter's night, with snow coating its dome, the effect is magical. You must've seen it on your descent Friday night. Whenever I'm flying into Montreal I know I'm close to home when I spot the Oratory's jade-coloured dome."

"Hadn't noticed."

When we left the cafeteria, Lucille stopped off at the adjacent pharmacy in order to buy a chocolate bar. I waited at the entrance. In both official languages, voices were raised. Lucille had gotten into an altercation with the cashier. I dashed over.

"*Qu-est-ce-qu'il y a?*" I addressed the cashier.

"*Elle ne veut pas payer!*" The cashier pointed to Lucille.

"She's trying to stiff me!" Lucille defended herself. "This bar costs fifty cents, and she wants six cents more!" A queue was forming. The people in the line were locals. They watched the exchange between the American tourist and the cashier. They kept quiet.

"It's the tax she's asking for," I informed my guest.

"What?!"

"Tax."

"Are you kidding?! There's tax on candy bars?!"

"There's tax on a lot of things." My tone was matter-of-fact.

"And you allow it? How can you let your government get away with a stunt like that?!" The high school principal was incensed.

"Well, it helps to pay for our medical care, for one," I answered blandly. Then I retrieved my change purse and placed six pennies on the counter. The image of a U.S. president was carved into one of them.

"*Ici.*"

"*Merde!*" muttered the cashier, as she scooped up the copper coins. "*Maudit americain!*"

I quickly steered the big black woman out of earshot before the francophone cashier spewed something worse.

The next day we drove to the Old City. It was swarming with tourists and locals enjoying, or enduring the last long weekend of summer. Cars crawled along the cobblestones. The air was oppressive. Lucille asked to make a stop at a tourist boutique. She bought T-shirts for her brother's boys. Behind us, another visitor grumbled, "It's hotter than hell up here. I'm going back to Florida!"

We were steps away from the St. Lawrence River. I suggested that we take a walk along the *quai.* "It's cooler by the river."

"No. I want to go back now."

"OK."

Lucille had booked her return for Tuesday morning, on the red-eye flight. I wrote out a recipe for yogurt herb bread, which she packed along with the T-shirts, and then she asked me to bake another loaf for her to take home. During supper Lucille told me that she had once been engaged to Muhammed Ali. Always accommodating, I pretended to believe her.

Early the next morning, in silence we rode to the airport. Lucille left. Light dawned. Traffic thickened as the city shifted into work mode. Students were rousing themselves to begin a new school year. I turned the wheel towards home. Summer was over.

THE PARTY'S OVER

Montreal, Quebec – The early winter of 1979

"Madam," the operator stated, "You'll have to end your call. You have an incoming call from a gentleman named Laurie, and he says it's an emergency."

"What?!"

"Madam, please disconnect your present call. I'm putting the gentleman on the line."

"Laurie, what the hell?! Why did you get an operator to cut into my line?!"

"I'm sorry, I had to do it. I'm on the emergency ward with Mark. There was an accident." There was a scream on the line. Laurie hurried his words. "But he's OK. He's OK. He got hurt in a hockey game."

"Oh my god! My boy! My poor boy! Where is he? Is he conscious? Can I speak to him?!"

"Sure. I'm about to bring him home." Mark's foot was in a cast, and he was outfitted with crutches. Laurie handed his buddy the receiver of the pay telephone on the emergency ward.

"Hi Ma."

"What happened?!"

Mark and Laurie winced as Mum's piercing wail ripped through the receiver.

"Nothing much, Ma. I stopped the hockey puck with my foot. The doctor says I have to stay off my feet for the next twenty-four hours, that's all."

Realizing her son would live, Mum recalibrated. It was Friday evening. Daddy and I were out shopping for ingredients for tomorrow night's party. Laurie was put in charge of the guest list, since he knew Mark's friends. It had been originally arranged that Laurie would keep Mark

70

out of the house the next day, so we could prepare for the party. The next day was Mark's birthday, and I was arranging this surprise.

Daddy and I returned from shopping before Mark and Laurie returned from hospital.

"Sit down, Abram," Mum commanded. "And don't panic. I have to tell you something." She did.

"Vot?! Why is Laurie in the hospital with him and not me? Why didn't he call me?!"

"He probably didn't want to upset you, Daddy." I knew my brother well enough to understand his motives. "Laurie would keep cool, and be able to help him better."

"Hunh!" Feeling rejected, Daddy grunted. "I am the father! *Mein* son is supposed to call ME!"

The next question was, how on earth were we going to prepare a surprise party if the recipient of the surprise wasn't able to leave the house?

"We'll manage," Mum affirmed. "We'll just have to work around him."

When Mark hobbled into the apartment, assisted by Laurie, he was pointedly ignored. Mum and I were in the kitchen, washing grapes and apples and plums.

"Why did you use your foot to stop the puck?" Incredulous, Daddy interrogated, as he and Laurie helped Mark into his room, relieved him of his crutches, and helped him into bed. "Why didn't you use your head?!" Daddy's crack was meant to mask his anxiety. As far as Mark was concerned, it didn't succeed in doing so.

Laurie joined Mum and me in the kitchen. "There are twenty people expecting to ring your intercom tomorrow evening around seven. What should I do?"

"Call them and tell them to stay away," Mum directed.

"You're going to cancel the party?"

"No no. Tell them to meet you downstairs in the lobby."

Generally nervous and impatient, Mum was masterful in crisis. "When we're ready, you can bring them up. And here," she tossed Laurie a package of deflated balloons, "take care of these. We can't put them up if Mark is here."

"Ma," I turned to my take-charge mother. "When and how are we going to bake the cake?" The odour of a cake baking would instantly arouse suspicion. Mum was a tigress when it came to protecting her cubs, but she wasn't cut in the Betty Crocker mould. Baking and cooking were luxuries reserved for women who had time for them. Mum's energies were poured into working with Daddy in the business they built together. Daddy was proud of his helpmate. He would brag, "Vot *mein* vife makes for dinner is – a reservation!"

"We'll have to do it after Mark goes to sleep," Mum decided. She was already splitting and pitting the purple-skinned, yellow-fleshed plums.

"In the middle of the night?" I was aghast.

"Maybe."

"Of all the days." I shook my head and wielded a small pair of scissors, snipping and separating bunches of blue-black grapes. "Mark has to stay off his feet for one day, and tomorrow has to be the day."

"Kiddo, it's a communist plot." Mum had done with the plums, and was coring Cortland apples. "But a good communist keeps going!"

Daybreak found Mum lighting matches and waving them around the kitchen in order to diffuse the odour emanating from the stove. The plum and apple cakes were cooling on the counter. Mum left the kitchen and knocked on Mark's bedroom door. "Sweetheart, are you awake?"

"No!" From beneath a thick quilted blanket, Mark moaned.

"Well you are now!" Mum burst into the room and extended her arms. "Happy birthday, my darling! Gimme a hug!"

"Ma, I can't." Mark extended his bandaged foot.

"Oh, right. Well, 'if Mohammed can't come to the mountain…' " Mum sat on the edge of Mark's bed, leaned over, and kissed him on the forehead. "What a beautiful morning!" She beamed, as sunshine filtered through the blinds and beamed with her. "My son is twenty-one years old today! Now if there's anything you need, you let me know and I'll bring it to you. How about breakfast in bed?"

"Sure, Ma." Injury had its perks. "Can you bring me a glass of orange juice, and a bagel with cream cheese?"

"If we don't have it, Daddy will go and get it for you. Now you just stay put and we'll take care of everything." Mark's room was located directly opposite the second bathroom. He needed to go no further, calculated Mum. My room was located at the far end of the apartment, off the kitchen and dining room. That's where the evidence would be stashed.

A tray of sliced, pungent cheeses was wrapped in Saran and hidden behind my typewriter. A bowl of plump grapes, both green and blue-black, was covered with a linen towel and tucked under my desk. Puff pastries, perched on the separated dividers of a silver serving dish, were balanced on the windowsill in my bedroom. Once the plum and apple cakes cooled, they were placed on large platters and slipped under my bed.

Mark, remaining in his pyjamas and a bathrobe, his injured foot propped on a chair, spent the day studying at his desk. Obligingly, he kept his door closed. Still, he heard the patter, and through the crack at the bottom of his door he could spy the movement of three pairs of functioning feet as they crisscrossed the apartment throughout the afternoon.

Before six o'clock, Mark limped into the hallway. According to Mark, Mum and I seemed to have grown heavier during the course of the day. My caftan and Mum's housecoat proved poor disguises for the finery we had on underneath. Daddy was still in casual dress, but then, Daddy was always in casual dress. Little short of a wedding or a funeral could compel the old socialist to put on a tie.

"I'm hungry!" Mark called. "Can I get something to eat?"

Mum and I were setting up a buffet at the dining room table. We nearly leapt out of our respective caftan and housecoat.

"Anything you want! In a minute! We'll bring it to you!"

Mark grinned. My brother was a good lad, and a bright one, even if he did stop a hockey puck with his foot. "OK. I'll wait." His grin spread, like the Cheshire cat, and he removed himself to his room, leaving the mice free to play.

The party was set for seven o'clock. It was almost seven-thirty and except for immediate family, the apartment was ominously empty.

"I'll go downstairs and see what's going on," Daddy volunteered.

In the main lobby of the apartment building, nineteen young people huddled on the steps, party horns in hand and at the ready. In a far corner Laurie's girlfriend sat quietly, her lips pursed and her cheeks puffed, intently blowing up and tying multi-coloured balloons.

"Laurie, why is everybody still downstairs? We can't fool Mark much longer." As if Mark had been fooled, at all.

"There's one guest missing. We're waiting for him."

"Why? He can find our name on the panel," countered Daddy. "Come outside with me. I've been cooped up all

74

day. I need air." Our cosy corner of North America was on the cusp of autumn and winter. Daddy stepped outside in his shirtsleeves, anyway.

"But its cold outside!"

"*Och*! You big baby! So vot! It's healthy! It's good for you! Come outside!"

Shamed into it, Laurie obeyed. Man, but Mark's father was tough. At that moment a red Porsche, its radio blaring rock music and its headlights blazing in the dark, careened down the street and skidded to a halt. A short, sandy-haired young man with a grin like a chipmunk hopped out, on the driver's side. His leggy blonde girlfriend tossed her golden mane, flashed her toothy smile, and emerged from the passenger side.

"Hi Laurie! I'm here!" the Porsche's owner shouted.

"Who the hell is that?!" Daddy's half-bare arms flailed in the chill night air.

"That's Marty." With his girlfriend Leslie, Laurie failed to add. "Mark met him last summer, at camp. Marty was Mark's supervisor. He was head counsellor."

"He's late." For Daddy, lateness denoted disrespect.

"Oh, Marty is always late." Already, those in Marty's orbit accepted that the rules which applied to them did not apply to him.

"So that is Schwartz's grandson." Daddy had heard of his son's new friend. Mark mentioned him a bit too often, for Daddy's comfort. Marty was the scion of wealthy *parvenus,* and heir to a textile empire. Daddy was aware of the family's shady reputation in business. A mischievous twinkle lit his soft brown eyes. His wife wasn't on the premises to recognize the warning light, and stop him. "Get outta my way."

Before Laurie could think, he had dutifully stepped aside. The heavyset, middle-aged man stomped his feet, like a horse, spit into his palms and rubbed them together, then sprinted down the street and leapt onto the hood of Marty's red Porsche.

"Hi!" Gleefully Daddy leered at Marty, who stood stunned. "I'm Mark's father. I'm here, too!" Daddy began to bounce on the car's hood and slap at it with his palms, eyeing Marty all the while. "Let's see how strong is this car. Let's see how much pressure it can take." Marty stood paralysed. Leslie stood transfixed. Laurie was no longer surprised by Daddy's pranks. He knew that, at some point, the man's motives would be revealed.

"Hok Kay!" Daddy leapt off the car, never letting his gaze leave Marty. "Looks like this car can take it!" Daddy extended his hand. "How do you do!" Marty raised his palm and dropped it limply into the older man's hand. Daddy slapped Marty on the back so heartily and shook his hand so hard that the younger man nearly toppled over. "So you are coming to the party?"

"Yes sir," Marty muttered.

"So come on in!" Daddy marched vigorously into the apartment building. Marty glanced furtively at the hood of his car, checking for scratches. Then he, Leslie and Laurie followed the leader, in silence.

As the evening's self-appointed master of ceremonies, Laurie directed the guests to the building's two elevators. Daddy bounded for the stairwell. "Mr. Fine, aren't you coming with us?"

"I don't take elewaiters. I take stairs."

"You're going to take the stairs?!" shouted Laurie's girlfriend, her arms filled with balloons. "But it's a long way up!"

"Are you calling me an old man?!" In Daddy's mind, the challenge had been issued. "Just for that, I'm going to take the stairs two at a time!"

Laurie shook his head, smiling at the gang. "It's OK. We'll meet him in the apartment." Laurie's girlfriend hung back, waiting until an elevator was free. Even alone, almost smothered by balloons, it proved a tight squeeze.

After climbing six flights one step at a time, Daddy estimated the young people had reached his apartment, so he ducked back into the hallway, hoping he wouldn't run into Laurie's girlfriend. As he sauntered down the corridor to his sixteenth floor apartment Mum stood with her hands on her hips, blocking his path. She was waiting for him, and she was ready.

"So where did you wander off to?"

"No where. The elewaiters was full. I took a later elewaiter."

"Sure you did." Shrewdly, she shook her head. "Showing off again, eh?" Mum knew her man. She also knew his sweetness. "Darling, you're not twenty-one anymore." She smiled, in spite of herself. "Now get inside, and act like a host!"

The guests were milling in the apartment. Several of the girls had taken to signing the cast on Mark's foot. Laurie's girlfriend trolled the apartment, rubbing balloons onto the walls until they stuck. Since the guests didn't know where to put their coats and jackets, they kept them on. One glance from Mum was all Daddy needed. He opened the hall closet and began distributing hangers. "Here. Here! Hang yourselves up! Make yourselves from home!"

After greeting Mark, who was sitting on one of Mum's high backed, petit point chairs like a monarch on a throne, the guests drifted to the dining table and helped themselves to the offerings at the buffet. Daddy had set up a makeshift bar, and appointed himself bartender. "Vot kind wine you want? We have all kinds! We also have cognac!" Daddy poured a dose of the burnt orange brew into a snifter, and presented it to Mark. "For you, *mein* son. You are old enough!"

Marty had recovered from the shock of his first encounter with our dad and was lounging on the petit pointed, cushioned, and aptly named loveseat. Leslie was in his arms. They were locked in a passionate embrace. Love is said to be blind, and the guests turned a blind eye to the display. Laurie's voice grew strident, and his jokey banter became strained. Mark grew fascinated by a vision on the ceiling visible only to him. I grew intensely uncomfortable. Mum ignored the couple necking in our living room. Daddy – did not. He went into the kitchen, removed a pitcher of chilled water from the fridge, opened the freezer and tossed ice cubes into the water, to chill it further, poured out a glassful and nonchalantly strolled behind the loveseat, a devilish gleam glinting in his warm brown eyes. This time, his wife WAS on the premises. Mum recognized the tell-tale signs. She launched into alert. "No!" Mum hissed, over the heads of the guests. Desperately she stage-whispered, "Don't you dare!"

Daddy hovered over Marty and Leslie while their tongues searched the insides of each other's mouths. The glass in his hand dangled precariously over their heads. Beseechingly, his eyes implored his wife for permission. By her fierce glare, he knew permission would not be granted. Dolefully Daddy looked down at the disrespectful couple, then longingly at the glass filled with icy water, in his hand. It was tempting. It was oh so tempting. Valiantly resisting temptation, Daddy lifted the glass to his lips and brushed the back of Marty's head with his elbow, instead. "You two should come up for air," he suggested, strongly, like a doctor. "It's getting hot in here." As Daddy's forearm grazed Marty's head, the younger man noticed the watch on the older man's wrist. It was a cheap watch, the kind worn by workers in his grandfather's factory. Marty sported a Rolex, on his wrist. Like a character out of Oscar Wilde, Schwartz's grandson knew the price of everything, and the value of nothing.

The evening proceeded with Daddy's approval. Laughter tinkled, and talk flowed. Gifts were unwrapped, photos were snapped, wineglasses were charged, raised, clinked, and toasts were made. Towards eleven the guests began drifting towards the door. Like a pasha, Mark leaned back on our mother's petit point cushioned armchair. He was slightly tired, and deeply happy.

"More apple cake, Ma! And a big, big glass of milk!"

Mum and Daddy were seeing the guests to the door.

"I'll get it for you." I went to the dining table and cut my brother a generous slice of his favourite cake.

As soon as the door closed on the last guest Mum's social mask dropped, and she whirled on Daddy. Mum and Daddy adored each other, but they didn't always understand each other.

"How could you? How could you?! How could you spoil your son's party in such a way?!"

"I didn't do nuttink!" Daddy protested.

Mark and I were blindsided by our mother's sudden attack on our father.

"Oh but you wanted to! You were thinking about it! And you would've done it too, if I hadn't been here to stop you! Your poor son, with his injured foot, and you would've embarrassed him and his friends by pouring cold water over their heads!"

Mark smirked. I giggled. Daddy struggled to keep a straight face, which served only to further infuriate Mum.

"And what about your daughter?! She worked so hard to create this surprise for her brother, and you almost ruined it!"

I interjected. "But Ma, I don't feel bad."

"You be quiet. I'm talking to your father!" I sunk back.

"Honestly Abram! I feel as if I have three children, and you're the biggest baby of them all!"

Daddy scratched his head, but the gleam in his eyes signalled that there were unplayed pranks still percolating in the spirit of the irrepressible jester.

"Ma, you're blowing this way out of proportion," Mark attempted to defend our dad.

"You go lie down!" Mum brooked no interference. "You need to rest your foot."

Mark lifted himself onto his crutches and hobbled off, to his room. Mum shook a fist at her bemused husband.

"I know you're laughing inside," she accused, "but you think about what I've said. You need to change your approach! Really Abram, you need to grow up!" Mum stomped off to Mark's room, to tend to her injured boy.

Glumly Daddy shuffled into the dining room. I trailed behind. Cake crumbs dotted the lace-edged tablecloth protecting the dining room table, and broken pieces of cake embedded with baked plums and slivers of apple lay abandoned on bone china dishes.

"I'm in the doghouse," Daddy pouted, like a reprimanded child. "She put me in the doghouse."

Like cool candles, the twinkling lights of the crystal chandelier, were reflected in a darkened window. It was Daddy's gift to Mum, once he could afford to give it to her. I removed the tea and coffee cups. Daddy removed the wine and water glasses and the silverware brought out only for special occasions. He carried them to the kitchen and rinsed them in the sink.

"We'd better wash these by hand, Daddy. They're delicate, and they might get hurt in the dishwashing machine."

While I washed dishes, Daddy dampened a small cloth, returned to the dining room, and used the cloth to wipe cake crumbs off the table, allowing them to drop into his free hand. He crossed back into the kitchen and kissed the top of my head, before tossing the crumbs into a plastic-lined garbage can.

"It bugs you, Daddy, doesn't it?"

Not talking meant deep thinking. I grew as pensive as my dad.

"Yes, it bugs me. I don't understand how *mein* son is finding such friends."

"I don't get it." I lathered and rinsed the china. Then I handed the dishes, piece by piece, to my dad, who now had a linen towel in his hands. "If strangers come into your house and they almost spoil your party and you want to do something about it, how does Mummy end up making you feel like The Bad Guy?"

"*Och! Mein shepsaleh!*" Daddy carefully dried the china and stacked them, dish by dish, on the kitchen table. "It's because I wanted to do something about it that Mummy made me into The Bad Guy."

"I understand you, Daddy." I picked up a second towel and wiped water droplets off the silver cutlery.

"I know you understand me." Daddy's gaze rested on my profile as we stood side by side, drying dishes. Tenderly he whispered, "Today is your brother's birthday, and you are the gift."

The party was over. As we tucked away the fancy dinnerware into the drawers of the large credenza Daddy relaxed, knowing he would live on in me.

81

PART OF THE FAMILY

The Laurentian Hills, Quebec – The summer of 2004

Mark showed up at my door. We escaped the heat and humidity of the city in mid-summer, and rode into the hills. Driving into a clearing, I emerged from my brother's air-conditioned SUV into a woodland paradise. The scent of pine and cedar assailed my senses. Marty and Leslie's country home was a log-panelled labyrinth large enough for two families who weren't talking to each other. They owned several hundred acres of surrounding land, on which they skied and ski-dooed in winter. To ease their aching muscles after such exertion, they built a sauna. Then they installed both an indoor and outdoor hot tub. Marty and Leslie also built a fully equipped, two-storey cabin at the far end of their lakefront property. They chose the spot because it overlooked a babbling brook. The cabin was their hideaway away from their hideaway. They used it when they wanted to escape their children.

A separate barn-like edifice was built several kilometres from the main house, accessible only by a winding dirt path, as storage space for the family's valuables. A pattern developed wherein a string of underpaid cleaning ladies, hired from the local village, addressed their grievances by casing the house they were hired to clean, and then sending relatives to rob it.

I came into the kitchen, where Leslie and Erin were preparing lunch. Leslie admired Erin, her older, more accomplished guest. Mark and Marty's wives got along as well as they did. Their children played peacefully together. The families travelled together on private bus tours and took turns hosting each other in their spacious homes.

"Hi!" I hailed. Leslie returned my greeting, which was more than she did with my phone calls. Erin did not. Erin no longer felt it necessary to acknowledge me. My sister-in-law had insinuated her way into my affections, and then recruited me in her campaign to conquer my brother. The clever woman staked her claim, and once her territory was secured she treated me with the particular contempt married women hold for hapless females bereft of male protection.

For Erin, the birth of each child brought with it an increasing sense of security with Mark, and escalating feelings of hostility towards me. Still, the physician my brother married showed restraint. It was always in private, always without witnesses, that she devised forms of humiliation meant to demean and demolish. After an initial period of shock and protest I withdrew, silently licking my wounds, in order to spare my brother a painful divide.

Leslie assigned a room to me where I could change into my bathing suit. I made my way down an incline, past the gazebo, onto the stone steps leading to an outdoor terrace, and further down to the private dock floating upon the lake.

Mark and two of his children were already there. Mark was lounging in one of the Adirondack chairs set up on the dock. In the morning, in the city, he bought three chocolate bars, to be divided among six children. Eleven-year-old Vivian, diving on and off the dock, had already gotten hold of a chocolate bar, whole. Now she wanted a second one. Mark told his daughter she would have to wait and share the rest of the chocolate with the other children. Like her mother, Vivian wouldn't share. She grabbed her little brother David under the armpits and held him over the water.

"If you don't give it to me now," she warned her father, "I'll throw him in."

David started to scream. "You're not getting it."

Raucously, Vivian laughed. "Give me the chocolate or I'll throw him in!" David squealed like a stuck pig.

"No."

Without hesitation, Vivian tossed David into the lake. He disappeared under the surface of the water. Vivian stared evenly at her seemingly impassive dad. David resurfaced, spluttering out the water he'd swallowed. The scrawny little boy tried to pull himself up onto the dock. He couldn't manage it.

"Help him, Vivian," Mark instructed her. Athletic Vivian pulled out of the water the little brother she had tossed into it. David, dripping wet, turned sad saucer eyes to his father, and dashed to him for comfort. Mark hoisted him onto his lap.

"We'll get her later," he whispered lamely.

"I'll kill her first!" David hissed, glaring at his sister from the safety of their father's lap.

"Vivian, that wasn't very nice." Mark was always a master of understatement.

Stunned into silence, from my deck chair I found my voice and ventured, "That was frightening."

"Well, I wouldn't go so far. It's not as if David can't swim."

I retreated into an increasingly familiar silence. There are few sights more daunting than a parent in denial.

Leslie called the children to lunch on the stone-inlaid terrace. Seductively, Vivian sidled past her daddy. The chocolate was forgotten.

"Love you, Daddy!" The budding beauty declared, as she sashayed up the steps to the terrace. Dejected little David dragged himself behind her.

Surveying the sunbeams darting on the glassy surface of the lake, Mark stated, as though I had dared to question his daughter's behaviour, "Vivian is going to make a great adult. She's determined, and she knows what she wants."

"I'm not sure she'll make a great adult, but there's no doubt she'll become a successful one."

Mark detected the note of sarcasm in my comment. He chose to ignore it.

"I'm going for a swim." I discarded my robe and plunged into the cool water, propelling myself to a tiny island that lay nearby. The surrounding water churned and seethed as motorboats roared along the shoreline. I noticed that beneath the surface of the water, my legs had taken on a toxic violet tinge. Returning to the private dock, I escaped the noxious fumes emitted by neighbouring boats, and climbed to the gazebo. The long rectangular table used for dining was occupied. A honey blonde head, bent over a sketchbook and art supplies, was visible through the screened-in door.

"There you are, sweetheart! I was wondering why I hadn't seen you before!" Rushing into the shady sanctuary, I enfolded thirteen-year-old Laura into my arms.

"Ooooh, you're making me wet!" Laura shook herself, like a shaggy dog.

"So what! I'm your one-and-only, ever-lovin' aunt!"

"Yeah yeah yeah." In spite of her protest, cuddly Laura smiled.

I plopped onto a plush, wide sofa, which was deliberately positioned to receive the sun. "Why weren't you with us on the water, sweetheart?"

"I don't feel like putting on a bathing suit." Mark's eldest had developed what is euphemistically referred to as "a weight problem". Self-consciously, Laura shrugged. "Please don't tell them I'm here. If they find me, they'll make me come out."

I looked closely at my niece. She had been a blissful baby, and a cheerful child. Now there were clouds in her sky-blue eyes, and a shadow fell across her sweet, innocent face. Carefully, cautiously, I began to probe. I discovered that my brother's eldest child could be as guarded as my brother. Like the recalcitrant top of a tin can, Laura began to open. She opened with a question for me.

"How come you don't have a husband?"

I, too, had learned to protect myself. To Laura, I told some part of the truth. "I never met the right man to share my life with. Looking back, I think I may have been too romantic. I couldn't bring myself to settle for less than my mother had."

"Where is Renia now?" My freewheeling mother was not a grandmotherly type. Everyone, including her grandchildren, called her "Renia."

"She's overseas, visiting friends." My mother Renia not only had friends, she had an international fan club. Only I seemed to know that Mum's vast social circle could never fill the hole nor heal the wound left by the premature death of my dad. His presence seemed to grow stronger, the longer he was gone. It seemed to me that since Daddy died, Mum had taken on aspects of his personality.

Laura looked away. Almost embarrassed, she stuttered, "They say I'm like you."

"Oh you poor kid! Is that what's been bothering you?"

Laura turned the blue pools of her eyes onto me, like lamps.

"Oh sweetheart." I reached out for Laura's soft, pudgy hand. "I can't promise that life will bring you a husband, though I expect it will bring you friends. I can tell you that you've already got something few people have."

"What is that?"

"Your art. Your talent. Your talent will be your lifelong friend. You can ignore it, avoid it, and take it for granted, but it will never betray you, and it will never abandon you. It will always be there, waiting for you to use it."

Laura's face brightened. Now it was her turn to study me. "How come you've got brown eyes, when everyone else in the family has got blue ones?"

"That's very observant of you." I mused. "Have you ever seen a picture of my dad?"

"Of course. Dad keeps a picture of him on his desk." "I know that photograph." I recalled. "I keep the same picture, and so does Renia."

Suddenly inspired, Laura flipped her sketchbook to a blank page, and began to draw.

I continued. "Do you recall the colour of his eyes from that picture?"

"Sure. They were brown. They had a twinkle in them. The colour of your dad's eyes was a warm, soft chocolaty brown."

As if on cue, from the kitchen the pronounced perfume of warm chocolate wafted through the gazebo's screens.

"Lana must've gotten back from her lifeguard job at camp," Laura commented, as she continued sketching. Lana was Marty's eldest.

"She said she was going to bake a cake for her dad's birthday party tomorrow." Thoughtfully, Laura gazed at me. "How come you aren't staying?"

"I don't know." I felt no need to cover for anyone. "You'd have to ask Marty."

Marty said your dad didn't like him when they first met." Laura must've been thinking about the dark-eyed grandfather she never knew. She had heard many stories about him. "How come?"

I grew pensive. "My dad couldn't dislike what he didn't know, but as an old socialist he was suspicious of Marty's background and nervous about the values reflected in his lifestyle. He was afraid of the influence it might have on his son."

"Hmmm." Laura pondered. "How did Marty feel about your dad?"

"Marty was a poor little rich boy who found a warmth and affection in our home that was missing in his own. Marty and my dad disagreed on everything, yet they came to respect each other. Still," I reflected on my father's ambivalence, while basking in the last rays of a lowering sun, "There seemed always to be a question mark floating over Marty's head."

"How old was Marty when my dad met him?"

"Mark and Marty met as counsellors in a summer camp when Marty was twenty."

"Marty used to be twenty?! He's going to be forty-five tomorrow!" It was difficult for the adolescent to picture their host as a young man.

"Sweetheart, we were all twenty once – or will be! Your birthday is coming up soon."

Laura tossed down her blue pencil, instantly upset. "Don't remind me!" The fragile girl was jolted. "I'm afraid to grow up!"

What could I say to her? I am not one to force-feed platitudes. "Sweetheart, when I was your age – even younger – I would talk to my future grown-up self."

"Huh?" Laura was intrigued. "How did you do that?"

"Well, I would picture what I had to say to her as a message I was inserting into a bottle. Then I would mentally toss it forward and think, real hard, *Don't forget me. When you reach the world of Tomorrow, don't forget who I was, who I am, and how much I hurt in the world of Today. Don't turn into someone who makes Nice-Nice and doesn't mean it. Don't turn into one of Them.*" I shuddered, startled by the memory elicited from me. "My younger self seems further and further away," I admitted, peering into Laura's pure, guileless eyes. "It's good that you're here to remind me."

Marty's beaming visage appeared in the screen of the gazebo. "There you are, young ladies!" Even on the verge of a birthday Marty is, and always will be younger than I am. "I'm taking the two of you on a boat ride!" It was not an offer; it was an order.

"Which boat are we taking?" I winked at my niece. In response, she rolled her luminous blue eyes. The question was almost a reasonable one. Marty owned six boats, after all.

"The biggest one, of course! My new six-seater!" Oblivious, Marty took me literally. "Get yourselves down to the dock. Laura, show your aunt where we keep the lifejackets."

Marty was a jovial host. As a lemony gumdrop of a sun melted into the hilly horizon, he took his passengers on a tour of the fir-fringed lake, its shoreline studded with luxurious dwellings ingenuously referred to as "cottages". The boat's motor carved a white, frothy wake through the water, and the wind whipped my cropped and greying hair.

"This is the life, isn't it, Noela!" Marty roared above the roar of the motor, satisfied, and self-satisfied. A captain at the helm of his vessel, he whizzed under bridges and sailed past Lana and Vivian, who were cruising on Marty's two-seater sea-doo.

"Come home for supper, girls! Enjoy!" Captain Marty ended the tour by treating his passengers to a self-created "toilet bowl" ride. He drove the boat in quick, vicious circles meant to simulate the flushing of a toilet. I grew nauseous. Gagging, I clasped a hand over my mouth in an effort to suppress rising bile.

"Marty!" Laura screamed. "Your driving is making my aunt sick! Cut it out!"

"Can't take it, eh?" Reluctantly, Marty slowed the boat

and drove it to his dock. I tottered to my feet and Marty helped me onto land. "I just wanted you to have fun," he came close to apologizing.

"It's OK. I did enjoy the ride, but now I gotta go lie down." I stumbled up to the gazebo, and stretched out onto a sofa wide enough for two people who were on very affectionate terms with each other.

Leslie and Erin were in the kitchen, preparing a massive salad. There would be two sittings; the first, for the children, the second, for the adults. The children were to be served first, in the dining room. Then Marty would morph from sea captain to cook, barbecuing outdoors on a propane grill, and on this soft summer evening the adults would dine in the gazebo.

Marty entered the kitchen, pressed Leslie against the counter, and nibbled on her neck.

"Not now," Leslie chided, attempting to shrug him off, though she didn't try hard.

"I brought in fresh berries and melons," Marty panted, as his hands travelled towards Leslie's breasts. "Is there anything else you'd like me to do for you, honey," he stage-whispered. "At least, before dinner?"

Leslie whinnied, maintaining a fine balance between embarrassment and pleasure. Erin bristled, pretending she had heard and seen nothing.

"Yes, there is." Conscious of an audience, Leslie's tone turned business-like. "The children aren't eating the fruit I put out for them. It's beginning to spoil. I want you to get rid of it."

"How?" Marty was more interested in ripe honeydews, than rotting raspberries.

"Oh I don't care!" Leslie tossed heedlessly, as she broke away and retrieved the canister of olive oil from the room-size pantry. The thick golden liquid was delivered directly from an Italian vineyard. "Give it to charity, for all I care!"

Clad in swimming trunks, with champagne flutes charged and in hand, Mark and Marty eased themselves into the outdoor hot tub, which was situated on a raised platform below the gazebo and the main house. Their flutes came to rest on the coaster-like indentations moulded into the tub's metal rim. Chocolate-coloured pots spilling over with violets were fastened onto the tops of poles standing sentinel along the sides of the tub. Massage jets whirred in the water, and tendrils of steam rose and evaporated into the early evening sky. According to the calendar, it was past the solstice, yet light lingered, as though reluctant to leave such a lovely place.

Laura, still refusing to put on a bathing suit, slipped into the tub, soaking her shorts and T-shirt, and not giving a damn.

"Dad, how come Auntie Noely isn't invited to Marty's birthday party tomorrow?"

Mark was embarrassed. Marty was not.

"Noela has to be in the city tomorrow." Mark quickly improvised.

"What for? She's a teacher! It's the summer holidays! Why do you have to drive back and forth four times in one day? It's not as if there isn't enough room here!"

Mark was fazed. Marty was not. He rescued his buddy from the girl's inconvenient questions.

"Look, Laura, it's what we've decided. Anyway, your dad loves his sister. He doesn't mind the driving. It's only one day out of a two-week vacation. Your dad gets to relax the rest of the time."

Marty turned abruptly, sipping on his bubbly *rosé*. Mark remained stone-faced. Laura mailed a mental note to her future grown-up self and me, who was eavesdropping from my vantage point in the gazebo, contacted the lonely child I believed I had left behind, assuring her that the messages sent so long ago had not only been received, but passed on.

I was returning to the city. Marty was coming along for the ride. I had been looking forward to private time with my brother. Once more, I was denied.

It was at dinner that Marty announced his intention to accompany us, which elicited vociferous protest from usually cool Erin.

"Oh you don't have to do that. It's late! You need your rest!"

"Mark is my friend." Marty slapped down my sister-in-law so fast and effectively that no one noticed, except me. "I want to keep him company on the ride, and I will."

This time it was Erin who was compelled to lick her wounds in silence. I was startled, and strangely relieved to discover that Erin perceived not only me but anyone close to Mark, as a threat.

Before leaving, we stopped by a clearing near a forest of pine. A bonfire was blazing in the playground Marty created for his children. Marty's boys had come in from camp on the eve of their father's birthday. All the offspring were gathered, extending broken branches capped with marshmallows to the edges of the fire. On seeing us Laura discarded her branch, picked up a thin package she had placed under a tree, and came running to me.

"Auntie Noely! I've got something for you!" Proudly, Laura presented her offering. "It's the picture I made in the gazebo this afternoon!" In the illumination provided by the fire, I could see the image of a young girl on the verge of womanhood. She had dark, shoulder-length hair, and her creator had given her navy blue eyes.

"Who is she?" I quizzed.

My niece beamed, her pale blue eyes radiant in the light of the flames. "She's your younger self."

"She's beautiful," I appreciatively purred. "But sweetheart, why did you give me blue eyes when I know you know my eyes are brown?"

"Well yes I know." To Laura, the answer was so obvious that she stated it impatiently. "But I wanted to make you look more like part of the family."

I was no longer accustomed to kindness. I batted back tears.

"I put the picture in a plastic protector so it won't get messed up in your bag. And see," Laura pointed to the bottom of the drawing. "I signed my name, like a real artist."

My moist dark eyes drifted to the lower right hand corner of the single sheet of sketchbook paper, on which was written, in big block letters, BY LAURA.

"Sweetheart," I affirmed. "You ARE a real artist." After a beat, I retrieved my voice. "I shall cherish this."

"I know you will." My niece recognized that I always said what I meant, or else I wouldn't say it. "Bye!" Laura sang, as she ran back to the bonfire, which was blazing, now.

The sky seemed to unlock like a jewel case set in indigo velvet. I raised my head, transfixed.

"Get in the car," Marty summoned.

Mark followed my gaze skyward to the panorama of celestial lights. "They're chunky, eh?" Mark entered the moment.

For the first time, I smiled a full smile. "You remember." As kids in summer camp, I stargazed with my little brother. "Look up at the stars," I had urged him. "See how chunky they are; like sparkly nuts in a chocolate bar!"

We rode through the woods, and out of the hills. I sat up front, next to my brother, while Marty lounged in the back. Ignoring the soundtrack of Marty's prattle, I kept my eyes on the stars.

After midnight, I was deposited at the front entrance of my apartment building. The two men came out of the car with me. Marty considered himself a gracious host.

"You're always welcome to visit whenever Mark is here." Mark winced. Marty grinned. He meant it.

"Ahh, thank you," I dully muttered, for Mark's sake.

Marty lifted my bag out of the car, and offered it to me. Mark snatched the bag out of his hand.

"I'm going upstairs with my sister, for a moment," he explained to Marty, as if chivalry needed to be explained.

"Oh good. Then you can take this too." Marty retrieved a large, heavy shopping bag from the back of the car. "I've got a present for you, Noela. It's a gift from Leslie and me." Mark relieved Marty of that bag, too.

"Why, thank you." This time, my expression was sincere.

Mark accompanied me into my apartment and stood uncomfortably, like a shy date.

"Is there anything I can do for you?" he mumbled. "Is there anything I can help you with?" His tenderness towards me was palpable.

"No. I can manage." I gazed into my brother's tired eyes, which were dark and blue like wild berries. "You'd better go. Marty is waiting and you've got a long drive back." Brother and sister were finally granted their private moment, and found they had little to say to each other. In lieu of speech, I reached up and embraced my silent sibling. "Oh my beautiful little brother," I thought to myself. "You made a good try." To Mark, I whispered, "Thank you for the day." Then I patted him on the back and sent him on his way.

A curious odour emanated from the kitchen table, where Mark had placed Marty's gift. I opened the bag, discovered its contents, and gasped. Inside was the turning fruit, no longer fresh, that Leslie refused to serve at their table. Disgusted and resigned, I lifted the bag and headed out the door, to the hallway incinerator. The image of my father, perched in a frame on my desk, stopped me in my tracks. His chocolaty brown eyes seemed to communicate his disapproval. Equally grim, equally mute, I hauled the rotting fruit to the incinerator. In vain, I wondered, "How did you know, Daddy? How did you know?"

FLAPPING PAST THE STARS

Melbourne, Australia – Christmas Time, 1999

"We can't let her leave like this! She's our guest too!"

"What should I do?"

"Go and get her!" Liza commanded her husband. Drew was phoning from his office. She had picked up his frantic call on her mobile phone. Liza was still at school, attending a Christmas party. It was the pre-holiday period, and Melbourners were in summer mode. A psychologist by profession, Liza worked as a guidance counsellor in a high school. Her difficult sister-in-law Ann had created another mess, and again it fell to Drew to clean it up.

For years my dead uncle's children encouraged me to visit them. In particular, it was my cousin Ann who urged me to come to her for an extended stay. Both Ann and I were unpartnered, and Mum was happy that her daughter and niece would finally meet and hopefully bond. Living in a different hemisphere, we had no idea what I was being drawn into, and those who did didn't bother to warn us.

After two weeks under Ann's roof I bit the bullet, and was on the verge of bailing out. I rescheduled my return flight, and called my mother in Montreal to tell her so. When my cousin Ann realized I was serious, she called in Drew.

To my Australian cousins my flight from Ann was a shock, but not a surprise. I had no way of knowing, and no one bothered to warn me in advance of my trip, but for Liza, too, Ann was anathema. Liza considered Ann a bludger, which is Australian for mooch. She was always barging into their home and demanding things. To Ann, a loan was equivalent to a gift. If Ann couldn't borrow what she wanted, she took it. If she couldn't take it then, Liza suspected more than once, she stole it. Drew had never been able to live in peace with his sister, nor had any other man, for any extended length of time. What the immediate family knew, and kept to themselves, was that Ann was a drug addict.

Obeying his wife's command, Drew left work and drove to his sister's house. There he discovered that I had rescheduled my departing flight for the next day. Ann, of course, had decamped. Always the injured party, no matter whom she hurt, Ann was consoling herself by getting stoned.

"My daughter Dana is on a student exchange program in France. She's unhappy there, but I told her to stick it out. You have to stick it out too," Drew uttered inanely.

"No. I don't." I was hot, exhausted, and beyond surprise.

My cousin Drew was unaccustomed to directness. He was a man who did not appreciate disturbance in his routine. Still, I had put up with Dana when he sent her to visit Canada, the previous year. He recognized that he owed me something.

"If you're determined to leave, we can arrange for the taxi to pick you up from my house." To this suggestion, I acquiesced. I am a teacher who scrimped and saved to be able to afford an extended stay in Australia. My dream, when finally realized, devolved into a nightmare.

We drove through the wide residential streets in silence. Angry tears trickled from behind my sunglasses. Still, I was able to distinguish and appreciate a light-coloured, bowl-shaped object bopping along the top of a hedgerow. The bowl flipped to reveal a woman's face. What looked like a bowl turned out to be a bonnet. The inhabitant of the hat wielded a set of clippers. She was tending her rosebushes. Every private garden seemed to lead to the next, in this aptly named Garden State. As we rode, a kaleidoscope of palms, fuchsias, hibiscus, teatrees and lemon trees whizzed past. From the window of a small music shop, the sound of a voice long stilled poured like dark syrup. The vocalized longing for an ideal world located over a mythical rainbow rose from a recording registered many decades past. The poster image of an adolescent, dewy-eyed Judy Garland sat in the shop window and flashed past my field of vision. Much to my cousin's discomfort, my tears flowed freely, now.

Drew drove up a quiet road lined with wattles and gum trees. In the front yard of a large split-level bungalow hung a forlorn-looking scarecrow. A pole was stuck up the back of its tattered shirt. Against the scarecrow in its cut-off jeans leaned a petite, pretty honey blonde. Liza and Friend were waiting in welcome. If I hadn't felt so defeated, I would've guffawed. The guidebooks were right. This really was The Land of Oz.

"He doesn't scare anything or anybody." Liza sighed in mock despair. "Truth be told, he's afraid of his own shadow. When his shadow shows up." Liza was referring to the blistering heat. The head of Liza's scarecrow drooped in assent. "But I love him just the same!" Liza slapped the back of the scarecrow, nearly knocking the straw stuffing out of him. "He's me mate!" Liza caught Drew's eye and smiled.

Liza knew she had caught Drew by default. Raised in a convent in Canberra, she fell in love with her future husband when they were both attending the University of Melbourne. Liza was drawn to Drew's glittering green eyes, which were hooded by double lashes longer and more luscious than a woman's. Before meeting Liza, Drew was involved with a pale blonde beauty who rejected him when she discovered that Drew's father was Jewish.

In the aftermath of the Second World War Drew had been Andrzej, and his sister had been Anja. There was still a hint of a foreign inflection in his speech. As a boy in The Old Country, Drew baited Jews. My uncle, who was my mother's older brother and, along with Mum, a survivor of Warsaw's infamous wartime ghetto, took Drew to the Jewish cemetery and introduced him to his ancestors. Shortly after, the family immigrated to Australia.

Liza was born in The Lucky Country, the only child of Polish Catholic immigrants who severed all pre-war ties. Drew distanced himself from his war-damaged family, and treated Liza's parents with more respect and consideration than he treated his own. However, Drew's generosity stopped at the edge of what he considered his family circle, which was immediate, and deliberately small. Now this stranger from another hemisphere was shuffling into their lives. I came into the cool shade of their hallway. What outrage had Ann perpetrated this time?

Liza sat me down at the kitchen table. Drew excused himself and withdrew. Liza put the kettle on to boil. "Have a cuppa tea, luv." Instantly cosy, we settled into the nook adjacent to the back garden, sipping on soothing camomile. "Will you tell me what happened?" Liza coaxed.

"I can't." My face crumpled. "She's his sister!"

"Drew is gone." The guidance counsellor in Liza emerged. "Just tell me."

Haltingly, I began. Sensing a sympathetic listener in Liza, I poured out a litany of wild abuse. When my confession was spent, we sat reflecting on the grotesqueness of the creature who had brought us together.

"I've suspected some of what you've told me." Liza

managed to mask her rage. She had been married to Drew for twenty-five years and never realized, until this moment, the extent of his sister's demoralization. Her heart reached out to the stranger who had been so savagely betrayed. A current of warmth crackled between us.

"Why don't you stay here for a bit?" Liza encouraged. "You're clearly exhausted. It will give you a chance to rest before embarking on such a long journey. Would you pay a high penalty for changing your flight again?"

I was starting to feel less insecure. "I came on an open ticket. I won't be penalized. But how can I do it? The airline offices would be closed by now."

"Only in Melbourne." There was a twinkle in Liza's warm brown eyes. "In Canada, today has just begun!" A very long distance call was placed to the Canadian Airlines office in Toronto. There was one flight available in a week.

Surrounded by my suitcases, I lay on a hastily made bed in an air-conditioned guest room, sipping the brandy Liza supplied. After two weeks in Ann's stifling townhouse, the cool air was a welcome relief.

Lightning sliced the dark sky and thunder rumbled in the distance, signalling the end of the scorcher and ushering in a change of wind that sent the temperature plummeting throughout the night. I slept fitfully. When I woke in late morning, the air was fresh and pure.

Rising in the silent and empty house, I began to explore. As promised, Liza left a spare key on the kitchen table, along with a hand-written note of orientation, and an open box of raspberry zinger tisane. I prepared a mug of the tart, fruity brew and took it outside into the back garden. There I discovered an oasis. Liza's garden boasted a hydrangea bush in full bloom, a plum tree, an apple tree, and a lemon tree. Almost every garden in suburban Melbourne bore lemon trees. Ann, with an addict's thirst, brought in lemons from the tree in her garden and squeezed them for lemonade, but I was not permitted to partake of the cooling beverage because, Ann chided, "Lemons take a long time to grow, and there won't be enough for me."

On Liza's lemon tree, its fruit dangled like Christmas baubles. As in the old song, they appeared pretty, but proved bitter.

There was a trampoline lodged at the far side of the garden. I dragged it to the centre of the open space under the lemon tree, and climbed onto its spring net. Listening to breezes wafting through boughs laden with fruit, I released my turbulent feelings into the unpolluted blue of the sky. A blimp floated overhead, belching white smoke that began to write on the celestial ceiling. Though it would ultimately spell out *Silverthorne Wine*, I half-expected the wispy letters to form into the admonition, *Surrender Dorothy!*

Liza took charge of the stranger in their midst. Though still at work for another week, she devoted every spare moment to me. She shopped for me during her lunch hour, returning home with little treats. Discovering that I love pineapple, a fresh pineapple greeted me in the kitchen each day.

Every afternoon I read in the garden or rested on the trampoline under the lemon tree, waiting for Liza to return from work. Liza began to see her environment through my eyes. I marvelled at the variety and abundance of local fruits and vegetables available within the same season. I declared the tap water as pure as spring water. I imagined gnomes and trolls residing in the gnarled, twisted trunks of the neighbourhood's towering, mystical trees. On a soft summer evening, as we dined *al fresco* on the downtown harbour front, the rectangular columns spaced along the embankment suddenly spewed gas flames. "O Great and

101

Powerful Wizard," I silently beseeched the darkening sky. "What deed must I discharge before going home?" In response, a flock of seagulls flapped past the stars.

Almost as soon as this idyll began, it began racing toward its end. I was the one who verbalized what we were thinking.

"If the December 30 flight is still available, I could stay another week. You'll be off work soon, and I won't be such a burden then."

"Oh I would love for you to stay!" Liza brightened. "As far as I'm concerned, you're welcome to stay as long as you like, but I'll have to consult with Drew."

"Of course." I suspected what Drew's response would be.

Drew scurried down the stairs to the kitchen, where I was squeezing the juice of a half-cut lemon into a large glass of water. For me, twisting off lemons from the branches of Liza's tree and bringing them indoors to make lemonade was a simple and rare treat.

"Noela." Drew's words were rushed. "I understand that you'd like to stay with us for another week, and at any other time of the year you'd certainly be welcome but," he hesitated, as Liza joined us in the kitchen. "If it were any time but Christmas." Liza's breathing was shallow and heavy. I was resigned. "I mean," Drew pressed on, "Ann joins us at my in-laws for Christmas dinner, and considering the bad blood between you, how would it look?"

"Ummm, the same way it looks now?" I ventured, dryly. Drew blinked. Accepting Drew's explanation at face value, I suggested a compromise. "You know, Christmas isn't my holiday. "I'd be content to stay here and enjoy the day under the lemon tree."

Drew winced. He disliked being reminded of his Jewish roots. "It's unfortunate that you don't have enough money to stay in a hotel." Drew bulldozed on. Liza's eyes darted daggers at him.

"I'm on a budget. I don't." I appeared matter-of-fact.

"Then it isn't do-able." Drew pronounced coldly, and with relief.

"No, it's not." I agreed, holding in my hurt.

"Perhaps it's best this way." Liza attempted to soften the blow. "If you leave on the 30th you won't be home until New Year's Eve. If there's a delay, you may find yourself still in the air at midnight."

"If I leave on December 30 I will arrive on December 30, since I will be flying backward in time." Then I looked Liza straight in the eye.

At six am on the morning of my departure, I stood by the screened-in door in the kitchen nook, packed, dressed and ready. I turned, and a drowsy, dishevelled Liza rushed into my arms. "You'll come back! You'll come back!" Little Liza whispered fiercely, hugging me close. For me, the only thing harder than leaving would have been to stay.

Liza stood on the curb in her housecoat and slippers, as Drew's car pulled away. I couldn't bear to look back.

Coming off the curb, Liza would later admit to me, she stopped on the lawn to commiserate with her scarecrow. "It's just you and me again, mate." The scarecrow's black button eyes glared at her in reproach. "Oh don't look at me like that! What more could I have done?!"

Through bleary eyes heavy with sleep, Liza saw the black thread stitched into the cloth head begin to twitch. "Are you trying to tell me something?!"

A mouth formed of black thread nearly burst its stitches

as it spit out its words. "You have more kindness than courage, my dear." The scarecrow was also a diplomat. "You will miss her more than you know."

"Well at least she gets to leave!" Liza blurted, finally saying what she meant.

As the scarecrow shook his cloth head, tufts of straw dropped from under his bush hat. Liza shuddered as he resumed his original inanimate position.

Foliage glistened as the sun rose over the trees and low terra-cotta roofs in this coral and emerald city. The magpies were chortling, and the currawongs were falling about from branch to branch. Dismissing the magic and evading the message of her vision, Liza bolted into the house and called Drew. "Did you see her off?"

"Well, she's gone." Drew's answer was open-ended.

"What do you mean?" Liza was instantly alarmed.

"I brought her to the Canadian Airlines counter and told her I was going to park my car, but she told me it wasn't necessary, she could find her way from there, so I left."

"You left her?!"

"Well, she told me to!"

I should have known. Liza blamed herself. She knew who and what she was living with. People always do.

Drew achieved the quiet he demanded, but the house was not at peace. During the holiday week, Liza dutifully accompanied her husband on a round of holiday dinners and parties hosted by his business associates. Late at night she lingered in the nook by the screened-in door to the back garden. The imprint of my form on the trampoline's spring net remained visible longer than one would have expected it to. On New Year's Eve, Liza again gravitated to the long sliding door at the back of her kitchen. Drew crept up behind her, and wrapped his arms around her waist.

"Darling," Drew hissed through his nostrils, as he nuzzled her neck, "why don't we take a trip up to Canada next winter? It will be summer there. We can visit Vancouver again." Liza trembled, fixing her gaze on the deepening shadows engulfing her lemon tree. She recalled that I live in an eastern province. The French one.

"From Vancouver we can arrange a cruise through Alaska." Oblivious, Drew spun on. "The ice and cold will make a refreshing change."

Drew's touch felt like tentacles crushing her spirit. Sacrificing me proved to be self-betrayal. Liza broke away from her husband's embrace. She entered her garden. "Don't go out there! You'll get bitten!" called Drew. The air was muggy and infested with mosquitoes. It was getting hot again, and this time it would stay that way until summer's end.

It seemed the entire world had come to Australia, since The Lucky Country would be seeing the new millennium first. Except for one rejected soul, who left it.

As festive fireworks flared over Melbourne's bay, Liza climbed onto the spring net of her trampoline, stretched out under the velvety night sky studded with stars as thick as the humidity, and awaited the arrival of the twenty-first century in the shadows cast by the lemon tree.

GUARDIAN ANGEL

Montreal, Quebec – The early winter of 1981

Aunt Ania was dying. Horrifically, Ania's children died before she did, but her abusive husband did not. My aunt Ania rose to heroic stature in wartime Poland, yet in peacetime she couldn't summon the courage to leave her brutish Belgian-born husband Camille.

During the four years she lived with and would die of cancer, my parents took care of my difficult aunt. My brother and I helped out. Mark accompanied Ania to early morning chemotherapy treatments before attending classes at medical school. I ran errands, directed by my mother. Ania pointed Mum to a safety deposit box in a bank vault.

"It's everything I have, and it's a lot. Use what you need to pay the expenses, and keep the rest for yourself."

When the box in the vault was opened, Mum stood aghast. One shiny copper penny winked at her, in mockery. Camille had reached the box first. The penny he left was his message to the two Jewish sisters he became entangled with when they were all slave labourers in wartime Germany.

Mum never told Ania of the theft. She assured her sister that she had retrieved the money, and then paid the expenses herself. During the last stage of her illness, Ania entered hospital and then screamed to be released because the doctors and nurses were bullying her, or so she claimed. After several days at home with her husband, Ania begged to be returned to hospital. The doctor in charge of the palliative care unit refused to allow her back so Mum hired a private nurse, wining and dining her and lavishing gifts on her, including Ania's fur coat, hoping she would treat her dying sister well and ignore the menacing presence of her brother-in-law. After accepting all the perks, the nurse stole Ania's jewellery anyway.

As Mum sat vigil by her dying sister, Ania gazed up and implored, "Finish it. Please finish it."

"What do you mean?"

"You know what I mean. There's no point in prolonging the agony. Please, *Renusia,* help me to finish it."

As the full import of Ania's request registered Mum recoiled and exclaimed, "No!" A part of her, the deepest part, questioned the extent of her love for her sister. Did she love her enough to help her die?

Ania overrode Mum's protests. "Cyanide. You can get cyanide."

"No! I can't. We're not in the Ghetto. There's no cyanide available here."

In the Warsaw Ghetto, a quick and easy death was the best one could hope for. Cyanide became an expensive and sought-after luxury. Ania had managed to acquire cyanide capsules for herself, but she would not share them with her younger sister. Though her feelings for Mum were ambivalent, Ania was determined that she be given every chance to live.

"There must be a way," Ania pleaded. "Camille trips me when I try to get to the bathroom. He's lacing the food with morphine."

"We'll find a way to keep you comfortable," was as much as Mum could bring herself to say. "But never ask such a thing again!"

"Abram, I want to get Ania out of her apartment. I want to bring her to us, to die."

"Absolutely not!" Daddy was unstintingly supportive during the ordeal of Ania's illness, but now he was drawing the line. "You will not bring Death into this house!"

"You're selfish!" Desperate to protect her sister, Mum reverted to the dirty street fighter she was compelled to become during the war. The accusation was unfair, and she knew it. Daddy always placed family first, and himself last. "*Oy chameleh mamaleh*!" Daddy switched into Yiddish. The words he used translate into Little Donkey Mother, in reference to Mum's stubbornness, but when Daddy used these words they became a term of endearment.

"I will do everything I can to help, but we cannot have the children disturbed. They need peace and quiet to concentrate on their studies. Especially Mark. He's going to be a doctor; he cannot be made upset by sickness."

As soon as the words tumbled off his tongue, Daddy recognized their irony. Mum smirked.

"Oh come on! You know what I mean!"

Frantic and overwhelmed, Mum burst into tears. Daddy wrapped his arms around her.

"*Kochana.* This is what I will do." Daddy negotiated. "Every day after work I will go to your sister's apartment. I will stay with her and make sure that animal doesn't go near her. She won't be left alone for a minute. I will sleep there, right beside her, on the floor in her bedroom, whether the nurse is there or not. Once the nurse is awake in the morning, I will go to my office." It was a remarkable offer. No one would've made such an offer, except Daddy. What Mum had long realized and Daddy never divined, was that Ania was in love with him.

Daddy kept his word. Each afternoon after closing his office, Daddy went directly to Ania's apartment. As soon as he stepped in Camille recoiled and kept his distance, eyeing his brother-in-law like a wary fox. Daddy was tender with women and tough on men, and Camille knew it. As long as Daddy was on the premises, Ania was safe.

Each evening Daddy lay on a mat, on the floor, next to

the bed where Ania lay dying. He would joke with her and sing to her and tell her stories that were almost bedtime stories, as he had done with me when I was a little girl. When the time came he would say the *kaddish* for her, the year-long prayers for the dead. In the meantime he served as her guardian and angel, until the Angel of Death relieved Daddy of his vigil, and released them both.

Ania spent her final days sleeping and at peace, lying next to the man she loved. Her sister had given him to her.

ON OCCASION THERE IS GRACE

Montreal, Quebec – The Mid-1970s

"Davida!"

From the back row of the dance studio a low, sultry voice responded, "Here!" My head swivelled. A long, leggy older woman lounged against a back wall, tossing her wavy red mane. I blinked in recognition. When my name was called, the redhead's reaction mirrored my own. Amid the staggered rows of young women clad in tights and leotards, standing barefoot, Davida and I eyed each other in the floor-length mirror lining the wall behind our teacher. Davida didn't smile.

After the class, returning to the studio's locker room to change and retrieve our gear, Davida's pace quickened as she rushed past. I stood quietly at my locker, contemplating the situation. Davida and I hadn't seen each other since my cousin Leo's funeral and *shiva* a few years before. Sighing, I decided. Enough is enough. Steadying my nerves, I walked over to the woman who pretended not to know me.

"Davida," I spoke softly, so our classmates wouldn't hear. "I know you know who I am." Davida's pale face grew paler. "Davida," I insisted. "I don't know what my aunt did to you, but whatever she did, I'm sorry!" Davida's cheeks flushed the colour of her hair.

"Davida." I knew I had her attention. "My mother feels the same way I do. She isn't mad at you. She feels bad about the way you were treated, but my aunt is sick now, my mother is taking care of her, and she doesn't think she can do anything about it." I felt no loyalty towards my nasty, cancer-ridden aunt. "Wait!" I ran back to my locker, fished for a pen and a scrap of paper in my bag, and then raced back to the flustered Davida. "Here!" I scrawled the family phone number. "Take it! I mean it. Call us! Call us anytime!"

Words emerged hesitantly from Davida. Then they began to flow. When Davida and I became comfortable with each other, we parted. On returning home, I heard my mother's voice in a one-sided conversation. Mum was on the telephone. She and Davida were revealing themselves to each other. I could hear Mum chuckling, gasping, sighing, and commiserating. I peeked through the door of my parents' room. The telephone cord was twisted around Mum's wrist. She waved me away.

"I'm talking to Davida!"

"Good!" I nodded approvingly. "Say hello from me!"

It was at my cousin Leo's wedding that I first encountered Davida. She was as striking as her name. Davida was exceptionally tall, and carried herself even taller. She had bright green eyes that sparkled like emeralds, milky white skin, and a shoulder-length mane of flaming red hair. She was open and eager to meet the guests who were about to become her extended family. A statuesque beauty, in high heels she stood almost level to the giant Leo. Davida was Leo's bride.

Their union proved a joyous one. The two young people loved their life together, and they were wildly in love with each other. Davida's parents and her younger sister were warm-hearted people who welcomed Davida's Chosen, and treated him well.

After her marriage, Davida continued her studies. She earned a teaching degree, though her dream was to be able to sustain herself as a working artist.

Leo was experiencing a sense of contentment, the first he'd ever known. In his teens, Leo's passion for football and his stellar performances on the field led to offers of professional contracts. On Sunday afternoons, in my aunt's kitchen, in awe I watched as Leo wolfed down two huge steaks before the game.

Aunt Ania prepared the steaks. After Leo's early

marriage, he abandoned athletics and set out on a sedentary path. But Leo's eating habits did not change, and his muscular bulk ran to fat. His coaches conditioned him to believe that large amounts of heavy protein were needed to maintain his strength. His mother fed but could not fulfil his appetite. Leo found himself trapped in a pattern he hadn't the will to break.

Davida didn't mind. The more man there was, the more there was to love. Leo's ballooning weight gave her an excuse to indulge her own appetite. The young couple became *gourmands,* basking in the glow of candlelit dinners, and in the loving reflection of each other's eyes. They so enjoyed the life they created that they felt no need to bring children into it.

Seven years into their marriage, Leo and Davida set off on vacation to Mexico. It was February. Leo was close to his twenty-ninth birthday. Halfway through their stay at a resort, nearing midnight, the couple were shimmying in a discotheque along with other vacationers, who bounced and sawed the air with their arms as though they were ringing bells. Multi-coloured strobe lights sliced jagged patterns in neon on the dark walls and spotlighted floor. Smoke emanating from legal cigarettes and the kind which used to be illegal wafted and intermingled above corner tables. In the rear, in shadow, a disk jockey spun records that were amplified through sound speakers. The falsetto wail of the Bee Gees thumping *Stayin' Alive* crashed through the club like ocean waves. Without missing a beat Leo lurched forward, fell on his wife, and slid to the floor. His heart stopped before the music did. The surrounding dancers laughed and turned away. They thought he was falling-down drunk.

Alone in a foreign land, it fell to the instantly widowed Davida to inform Leo's family of his sudden and massive coronary, and to arrange the return trip to Montreal with a 350-pound corpse.

Aunt Ania had never been kind or pleasant to Davida. Casting for a scapegoat to lash at for the loss of her son, she targeted her defenceless daughter-in-law.

"You killed him!" Ania shrieked, immediately after the funeral. "You made my son eat! You dragged him to fancy restaurants and made him pay for your pig-outs! He didn't get fat until he met you. If not for you, my son would be alive!" The accusation was illogical and unfair, but logic and fairness were never Ania's strong points. The intention was to demolish her daughter-in-law because she was alive and Leo wasn't. It worked.

In Ania's house, which had become a *shiva* house, audible gasps erupted from Leo's former highschool classmates when my sixteen-year-old brother Mark walked in. They had never seen him before. There was no clear resemblance between the features of the oldest cousin and the youngest, but Mark had the height, the high and wide Slavic cheekbones, the slanted blue eyes, the blondness, and the big-boned bulk of the buddy the mourners remembered from their teen-age years. It was painful for Davida to look at Leo's young and lively cousin. It also gave her consolation, of a kind.

In the aftermath of Leo's death, Davida uprooted herself and resettled in Toronto. Her younger sister was there.

"I'm sorry to see you go," I told her, during one of our frequent phone calls, "but I understand its best that you make a fresh start." My loss was magnified when Mark moved to Toronto, too.

In a new city, Davida built a new life for herself. Many men would visit her bed. Too many, I mused, but then, who am I to judge? When you find what you're looking for, you stop looking. When you lose it? What then? Davida was candid about her sexual affairs with married men. It seemed she deliberately got involved in dead-end relationships in order to avoid the risk of falling in love again.

Thirteen years after Leo's death Davida decided to break through a self-imposed barrier, and went on vacation in winter. At forty-one she hadn't remarried, and never would. On her own, she chose to go to a Caribbean resort. In February.

Halfway through her two-week stay Davida was sitting at a counter in a bar, an untouched drink in her hand. She was watching the clock that hung high above the rows of glasses. The hands of the clock were nearing midnight. It was minutes away from the moment of Leo's passing. Davida willed herself to sit still and breathe through it. As the large hand of the clock continued to tick, a young man in his late twenties entered the open door. He looked like a gentle giant. He had high and wide Slavic cheekbones, slanted blue eyes, and carried his big-boned bulk lightly. His apparition-like appearance tipped Davida into a parallel universe. The young man wasn't attuned to the cosmic forces that had merged and steered him into this particular bar on this particular island on the anniversary of his cousin's death. But he recognized Davida instantly, as if no time had passed since the *shiva* and this moment. Like a friendly ghost, he greeted her. "Hello Davida." Mark's fiancée was with him.

Davida returned Mark's warm gaze, noting his blueberry-hued eyes, the inquiring tilt of his head and his quizzical grin, so achingly reminiscent of the man she had loved and irretrievably lost. For the remainder of Davida's stay the threesome kept company, sailing and swimming and dining together. Leo's Beloved wasn't alone, anymore.

Returning to Toronto, Davida got involved in Mark's

wedding plans. She designed and painted the invitations by hand. Davida, Mark and I would once more dance at a family wedding.

As their paths diverged, Davida fell out of touch with my brother and his bride. She was busy carving a career. She didn't lack friends. My brother was busy not only building a career, but also with raising a family. Living four hundred miles away, I was the one who kept the line open with Davida.

"Are we relatives?" I asked, during a long-distance call, "or are we friends?"

"Oh, we're friends!" Davida was emphatic. "If we were relatives, I wouldn't be talking to you!"

I delighted in hearing of Davida's triumphs. "I go to a dance class every night, and then I come back to the apartment, rest in a tub filled with bubbles, and soak my feet under the mix of cold and hot water running from the faucets. It's comforting. It cuts my appetite. I've lost twenty pounds!"

Davida's efforts in her professional life were paying off, too. She was taking on less tutorial work. Her paintings were beginning to sell. Davida was making a name for herself, and the name being established was Leo's name. As independent as she was, Davida never relinquished her married name.

Briefly Davida would return to Montreal to bury her mother. We met in a café. Her appearance was shocking. Obesity distorted the features of her once-lovely face. The flaming red mane, which had darkened to the hue of burnished amber, was gone. There were a few strands of hair clinging to her head. She seemed to be heavily medicated. We couldn't find much to say to each other. Davida recognized how distressed I was by her appearance.

"I've been through a tough time," is all the toughened

Davida would admit to. It was rumoured, and seemed true that Leo's widow, now middle-aged, was battling breast cancer. The only recognizable features were her emerald eyes.

One afternoon in early spring, when tender, budding leaves lace the sky a primavera green, I was descending the hill of Montreal's central nature park when a statuesque redheaded teenager appeared in my path. The girl was jogging up the hill. Her climb had just begun. She was fresh-faced, innocent and lovely. As the girl pranced past she favoured me with a sweet smile. Pain inflicted in the distant past surfaced in my restless mind. Returning to my apartment, I looked up Davida on the Internet and quickly found news of her, in Toronto's *Globe and Mail*. The item was several months old. It was her obituary. The first line began, *At North York General Hospital, beloved wife of the late Leo Heise...* I blanched. Davida's sister must have placed the notice, I thought. There was no other kin left to do it... *Loving sister and sister-in-law... and dear aunt...* Recovering, and re-reading the manner in which Davida's surviving family chose to represent her, in spite of the news, I smiled.

OUT WITH THE OLD

Montreal Quebec – The New Year of 2004

For my mother Renia, New Year's Day was the hardest day of the year. Her mother died on New Year's Day. As long as Dad was alive Mum was able to endure January first, but after he died she took to sedating herself in order to sleep through the day. After Dad died I never left Mum alone at the start of a new year. My brother Mark escaped to the ski hills with Marty.

As the years went by, my steady presence calmed Mum, and she was able to keep herself conscious on New Year's Day. On New Year's Eve, Mum kept vigil by her window until I appeared. Regardless of the weather, I always appeared.

Before his marriage, Mark relocated to Toronto. He saw Mum on her visits to Toronto during holidays when work prevented him from coming to Quebec to visit Marty. Mark saw me when a tribal celebration dictated he couldn't get away with inviting Mum without inviting me. If the celebration was large enough and I could be seated far enough out of her sight, my sister-in-law Erin managed to tolerate my presence.

Early one winter, I let Mark know how painful the start of the year was for our mum. Mark and his family were coming to Quebec for the Christmas holidays. They had been invited to spend Christmas week at Marty's country home in the Laurentian Hills. Mark's response was to ask Marty if he could bring us with him so we could be together on New Year's Day. Marty granted us permission to spend New Year's Day together. Just the day. He wasn't keen on us staying overnight.

Early winter was raw and bitter, that year. The snow was still white, but the ice was black, and the roads leading up north were treacherous.

Originally we were a two-car family, but Mum gave the younger and better car to Erin as a wedding gift, and now the car Mum had kept for herself was too old and decrepit to make the trip. Under such conditions it would've been gruelling for Mark to make two round-trips in the course of one short day. Mark's solution was to arrange for Mum and me to stay in a hotel in Ste. Agathe. He could go skiing during the day and bring us to Marty's home for dinner. After dinner he could return us to the hotel and deliver us to Montreal the next day, his duty fulfilled.

Before booking the hotel room, Mark broached the idea to Mum.

Pride and pain overwhelmed her, as she mentally walked through the visit Mark planned.

"You jerk!" Mum didn't mince words. "If that friend of yours can't be bothered to call and extend the invitation himself, I don't want to hear you acting as his messenger boy! You don't need to stick your old mother in a hotel. I don't need favours! The two of you can go skiing and go to hell!" Then Mum echoed my dead dad. "Do it right, or don't do it at all!"

Before Mark had a chance to respond, Mum slammed down the receiver. "Shit!" Tears pricked her eyes. Almost violently, she swiped them away. "I'm not going to become one of those old mothers who gets taken out of moth balls once a year. They can do what they want the way they want, and to hell with them!"

I sighed. "It's alright, Ma. We'll do what we always do. We'll hang out together. If it isn't too cold we can go to the park. In the evening we can go to the movies. It's alright, Ma. We'll get through it."

There would be no walk in the park on New Year's Day, and no going to the movies. As if to ensure she wouldn't be going anywhere, Mum wrenched her back.

"Just because I'm in pain doesn't mean you can't go and be with your brother! Go! Go up north and have a good time!"

I shook my head. My mother was a damaged war orphan constantly testing her children.

Mum spent New Year's Day in bed. As I massaged and kneaded her knotted muscles, under my hands I could feel her reliving each moment of the events leading to her mother's death. In the bombardment of memories, once again she was terrorized by the siege and occupation of Warsaw. Once again she was a young girl dispossessed by German occupiers. Suddenly homeless, Mum's security and innocence and ability to trust were destroyed. In memory, over and over, she suffered the deterioration of public sanitation and public morality. Again she inhaled the stench of rotting horseflesh, as a starving urban population attacked and consumed animal carcasses in the city streets. The waters of the Vistula River became contaminated, creating the first wartime epidemic of typhus. Once more my mother Renia was a terrified eleven-year-old watching, in helpless horror, as the disease attacked and consumed her mother at the dawn of 1940. A portrait of Mum's mother, an enlargement of the only image she was able to save, gazed silently from the wall above her bed.

As I eased my mother's cramped muscles, I reflected. If bringing us up north was too complicated, why didn't Mark take a day out of his vacation and come to us? The driving would be halved. He wouldn't have to stay in a hotel. Mark was always welcome in his mother's home.

As I massaged and then served snacks and tea, Mum gazed longingly at the telephone lying mute on her nightstand. Mark didn't call on New Year's Eve, nor did he call on New Year's Day. He didn't call the next day. Mark broke his silence on January third to announce that he would be passing through Montreal on his way home and intended to drop by. After her son's punishing silence, Mum was duly chastened and grateful.

"The food! The food! They're coming for lunch! I'm going to get to see my grandchildren. Hurry up! What am I going to cook?!"

The worst of Mum's back spasms had passed, but she was still stiff. "You're not going to cook." I vetoed the idea. "Neither am I. I can help you bring in provisions and set a table, but that's all."

In the old car we shared, I drove Mum to the supermarket. Mum and I shared everything. We shopped and I carried the groceries into her apartment. Mum brought out the fancy china stored in the large credenza, and I unwrapped and placed on serving dishes sesame seed-studded bagels and cream cheese and smoked salmon. In the dead of winter tomatoes were egregiously expensive, but on this occasion, for this occasion, Mum purchased them anyway.

"Don't forget the orange juice!" Mum trilled. Dutifully, I poured orange juice into a large jug and set it, like a centrepiece, on the dining room table. "It looks lovely!" Mum approved the spread. "All of Mark's favourite foods!"

Only after Mum brought out the silver cutlery and set them on linen napkins did she consider the table ready. She sat vigil by her living room window in anticipation of Mark's arrival, as she sat vigil on New Year's Eve, waiting for me.

When the buzzer rang, Mum almost jumped. "They're here! They're here!" She rushed to the door, heedless of her aching back.

Mark, his wife Erin, and their trio of children trooped into Mum's apartment, shaking the snow off their jackets, and shaking off their boots. After their skiing holiday, they were relaxed and happy.

"Hi! Happy New Year!" The children greeted their grandmother and me. Erin acknowledged Mum, and ignored me. Erin always ignored me.

"I'm leaving," I announced. "I need to get groceries into my own fridge. I have no food."

Mark seemed surprised. So did his children, but they shrugged off my precipitous departure, and headed to the dining table to devour the spread their grandmother had prepared for them.

I climbed the slope to my neighbourhood grocery store. Holiday lights twinkled in shop windows. Ice pellets, sharp as needles, struck the hood of my jacket. The temperature had risen, and falling snow was transforming into freezing rain. Particles of ice formed on the bare branches of trees lining the sidewalks, transforming them into ghostly, glistening chandeliers. At the grocery store I arranged for a home delivery. Then, gingerly, I made my way down the slippery slope.

Inside my apartment I lined the living room floor with old newspapers.

"Happy New Year!" hailed the deliveryman, in anticipation of a generous tip. "Ah ha! The Yellow Brick Road!" The deliveryman clumped along the road of old newspapers, grocery box in hand, set down the box on the kitchen table, and clumped back out again.

"Happy New Year," I recited, and placed the prepared tip in his proffered hand. The deliveryman departed, and I scooped up the soiled newspapers. An article caught my attention. I stood in the middle of the living room, reading it. Harshly, the telephone rang.

"How could you?!" Mum lashed at me because I would

take it, and Mark wouldn't. "How could you hurt your brother like that?!"

"What?!" I dropped into an armchair, a piece of soiled newspaper in hand.

"You left! You just left! Your brother came to visit with his family, and you walked out! How could you be so rude?! Your brother was hurt, and the children were upset and confused. And what kind of an impression do you imagine you made on your sister-in-law?!"

The stunning injustice of Mum's attack left me defenceless.

"Oh come on, Mum. You had a sister-in-law, too. In her eyes you could never do anything right. Surely you remember what it feels like to look bad, no matter what you try to do." Bitterly I added, "I'm sorry you're disappointed in me. But you're not the only one who's lonely. I'm lonely, too. And it hurts."

Mum gasped. "Sweetheart! I didn't say I was disappointed in you!" Mum heard what she wanted to hear, and she was never defenceless for long.

"All I said was that you should consider your brother's feelings and try to be more accommodating. Why do you begrudge your brother his vacation? He works hard. He needs it. You should be happy that your brother is happy. How can you be so selfish." Mum wasn't posing a question. On this subject, I wasn't going to get heard. Despairing, I conceded defeat. "I can't deal with this now, Mum. I'll call you later." I dropped the receiver and tossed the soiled newspapers into the trash. Longing for my father and fighting back tears, I moved heavily into the kitchen and put away the food.

"TODAY I AM A MAN"

Mississauga, Ontario – The autumn of 2004

It was the highlight of Mississauga's social season. In a
boutique hotel, the main reception hall had been booked
two years in advance. Caterers, florists, a rock band and a
group of dancers, some holding day jobs as aerobics
instructors, had been engaged months in advance. The guest
list topped two hundred. Many of the guests would be
coming from out of town, including Marty, Leslie and their
brood. When Mark discovered that, upon arrival, Marty
paid the bill on his suite, he contacted hotel management,
cheerfully bullied them into giving his friend a refund, and
paid the bill, instead.

I was surprised to see Leslie at the event.

"Don't judge!" Mark snapped. "You don't know how
you would behave under the same circumstances. People
need a break!"

"I'm not judging." I was defending myself. I seemed to
be on the defence a lot, these days. "I just don't understand."
Leslie's father was dying of cancer. He had been given a
week to live. Under the circumstances, how could Leslie
justify leaving his side in order to travel four hundred miles
to attend a birthday party? Surely, she had the rest of her life
to take a break.

It was the Canadian Thanksgiving holiday weekend.
Mum and I flew in on Friday night, and were installed
in a deluxe room Mark arranged for us. I was noticing a
change in my mother. She tired easily. Too easily. She
was spending an inordinate amount of time in
bathrooms, straining over toilets. Spending the night
with her in this deluxe room with twin queen-size beds,
I became aware of Mum's marked flatulence. Dare I

123

point it out to her? Who else could she hear it from without feeling humiliated?

"Mum, what are you eating these days? Do you get enough roughage?"

"You know I always eat big salads, and I put flaxseeds in them, too."

"Then why are you having digestive problems?" I asked, lifting a Crispin apple from the large fruit basket Mark had sent to our room.

"I guess it must be because of the haemorrhoids. Dr Stein keeps cutting them out of me, but they keep growing back. At least, I think they are. They must be. Dr Stein says he can't see them anymore, but I'm still bleeding." Mum sighed. "I'm going to see him again in two weeks. I'll ask him to arrange another colonoscopy."

"You're going to see him on your birthday?"

"It's my gift to myself, sweetheart. I want to be healthy." Mum trusted the colon rectal specialist. Mark had gone to medical school with him. I trusted that the people most precious to me knew what they were doing.

On Saturday morning, a ceremony was held in the synagogue. My nieces were fourteen and twelve, respectively. This was a double *bat mitzvah*. When my brother married a Gentile he began to take seriously the fact that he is a Jew. In Canada in peacetime, having reached the age of thirteen, or almost, my nieces were going to be confirmed under Jewish law. Under Reform Jewish law, at least.

Reaching the age of thirteen was not always as easy as it seems. The death of a child is difficult to comprehend. The murder of a child is incomprehensible, yet by the time Mum reached Laura's age she was one of the last child survivors of a murder machine. At Mum's request, Laura and Vivian entered into a ritual called "twinning," in which the grandchildren of Holocaust survivors about to be confirmed join with the ghosts of children who never reached confirmation age. While Mum sat quietly imploding, Laura read from a prepared text.

"At our *Bat Mitzvah* of remembrance, we wish to honour the memories of Tolek Pomeranc and Rysia Oksenberg. Tolek was twelve and Rysia was nine years old when they were murdered in Treblinka in August of 1942. Rysia never had a chance to go to school, so Tolek and our grandmother tutored the little girl. She had big beautiful blue eyes and curly blonde hair and wanted to be a ballerina when she grew up, except that she wasn't given the chance to grow up. Her parents nicknamed her 'Shirley Temple', an American child movie star who was very popular in Poland."

Mum had prompted Laura well.

"Tolek was a little scholar. He was short for his age. He wore glasses and always had his nose in a book. He wanted to be like his father, a well-known journalist who wrote under the name Marek Pomer. The last glimpse our grandmother had of her cousins was when they were being pushed onto the platform of an open truck."

Mum bowed her head, and slipped into a parallel universe.

"Rysia and Tolek never had the opportunity to celebrate their *Bar* and *Bat Mitzvahs*." Laura stated the obvious, and then pronounced, "May their memories be blessed forever."

The congregation sat silent, contemplating the greatest attack on children since Biblical times. Mum ached with sadness. She had made it her mission to transmit memory. On this crisp Saturday morning during a Thanksgiving weekend in Canada, she believed she was succeeding.

After the ceremony a luncheon was held in the synagogue, and then the guests retreated in order to recover, regroup, and prepare for the evening's event. In many cases this meant getting one's hair done, or redone. In my case, it meant going outside and getting what my dad would call "air". I invited Mum to join me. She declined. "I need to rest, sweetheart. I'm tired."

"This isn't like you, Mum."

"I guess my age is catching up with me. I'm not the superwoman you take me for. I know you don't want to see it, but I'm old enough to be dead."

I shuddered. It was true. I couldn't tolerate signs of physical decline in my mother. To me she was invincible. She had to live forever. I insisted on it.

I left my Mum resting in the deluxe room on the third floor and went out to walk alone. Our boutique hotel was nestled in a village by a lake. Restlessly I marched up and down the boardwalk.

In the evening, in my finery, I remained alone in the deluxe room on the third floor until pounding rock music in the main reception hall blasted me out of it.

"There you are! I was just coming to get you!" As I stepped out of an elevator and into the lobby, my brother greeted me. His wife was greeting guests at the entrance of the reception hall. She looked lovely. Erin was wearing an off-the-shoulder, baby blue-coloured ball gown that complimented her pale blondness.

"You look really nice!" My brother examined my sage green gown, and complimented me sincerely.

"You look like a baby blue penguin," I blurted. Under his tuxedo, Mark was wearing a waistcoat the exact colour of his wife's gown. With his darker complexion and massive bulk and height, the pastel shade made him look sick.

"You know," Mark pouted, "if I were sensitive like you, I might be hurt by that remark."

"Then it's lucky for you that you're not!" *Bloody hell.* My lips curled. I tasted foul-smelling chemicals as amber-coloured lipstick seeped onto my tongue. *Those two should be perched on top of a multi-tiered cake. Barbie Doll is turning my brother into a Ken Doll. And he likes it.*

At the entrance of the reception hall, the evening's celebrities were preparing to make their entrance. The entrance was wide enough for Laura and Vivian to walk in together. Still, Vivian shoved her older sister out of the way.

"You don't have to push me!" Laura pouted, rubbing her arm. "I'll go second, and I'll go quietly! You can go first! I don't care!"

Laura felt my eyes on her. "Vivian's always got to hog the spotlight!" My generally gentle and accommodating niece erupted in frustration.

"Yes sweetheart. I know."

"She always has to come first and be first and get all the attention! Everyone thinks she's hot stuff, but she always sets me up to make me look bad."

"Not everyone, sweetheart." Laura's position was one I understood too well. "Don't underestimate the audience. Not everyone is stupid." This was cold comfort to a fourteen-year-old.

"So she can have all the attention." Laura didn't seem to hear me. "I don't care!" Laura cared a lot.

With a toss of her finely shaped head, Vivian dismissed her sister's outburst. The girl had star quality, and knew it. On the evening of her confirmation Vivian was wearing a backless, low-cut, smoky grey-coloured gown. The garment rested easily on her budding and braless breasts. The sides of the gown were slit up to her burgeoning hips. The girl had applied smoky grey shadow to her eyelids, and strutted in stiletto heels. Disconcertingly, the twelve-year-old looked twenty.

Fourteen-year-old Laura wore a modest pantsuit of her choosing, and pumps with high heels she had been pushed into by her mother.

"My feet are killing me! I can't stand these stupid shoes!" Laura hobbled into the hall, on the spiked heels of her glistening sister. I followed. Place cards were set at the round tables spaced throughout the hall. I searched for my place, and found it relegated to the side with the children's former nanny and her male companion. At the largest round table, which served as the table of honour, Marty and Leslie were seated with Mark and Erin, as if they were family. Erin glared at me, slit-eyed. The phantom of Auntie Stalin hovered behind her. I lowered my head, bit my tongue, and vowed to have a good time, anyway. Daddy wasn't there to tell Erin what he thought of her seating arrangements. Or was he?

After dinner, we were subjected to a curious kind of slide show. Photographs of my nieces from infancy to adolescence were projected, cinema-size, onto a wall. The last image to appear was that of a man most of the guests never knew, and never would. I gasped, squeezed my eyes shut, and my head dropped backwards as if I had been shot. When I looked up, the movie screen-sized image was gone. Then it leapt back onto the wall.

The warmth of the image's smile and the mischievous twinkle in its eyes hovered over the heads of the mystified guests like the Cheshire cat. Mark introduced what appeared to be an ambivalent ghost.

"This is the only guest who is missing. He's my dad." So saying, Mark burst into tears. Mum rushed over from the table where she was seated and threw her arms around him. So did I.

"Mark, what happened? Was it my imagination? Daddy disappeared – and then he came back!"

Sniffling, Mark explained. "I planned to show that picture last. I was looking for a way to have Daddy here, but I didn't want to talk about him. I was afraid if I did, I'd break down."

Mum and I chuckled, and affectionately rubbed Mark's back.

"Yeah, well." Mark could appreciate a joke, even when the joke was on him. "All the other photographs were timed to stay on for three seconds and then go on to the next ones, but Daddy's picture was supposed to come on and stay on. I don't know what happened. The projector switched itself off, so I went and turned it back on."

I should've known that being dead wouldn't prevent Daddy from expressing his opinion. Ruefully, I eyed Mark.

"The projector switched itself off? You don't really believe that." I smirked. Mark's eyes popped. I shook my head. My brother, the doctor, doesn't believe anything he can't see on an X-ray. Poor man. He misses so much.

Rock music was blaring. It was impossible to carry on a conversation, so I got up and danced. As I shimmied on my own, the flashing strobe lights seemed to materialize into a human silhouette as one of the hired professional dancers leapt off the stage and joined me.

"You're cute!" The young man shouted. Impulsively, he kissed me. My unintended conquest didn't go unnoticed. Vivian has built-in radar for competition. She honed in and actually spoke to me.

"Gee, you're a good dancer. Who knew you could do anything."

Nine-year-old David noticed too. My nephew loped across the crowded dance floor, shaking empty *Seven-Up* bottles like a set of maracas and shouting out, to the amusement of guests scattered among the round, cabaret-style tables, "We are family! I got all my sisters with me!

We are family! Get up everybody and dance!" Cutting in on my partner, David commanded, "She's my aunt! I'm dancing with her now!"

My nephew has inherited my sense of rhythm. We gyrated and bounced and bumped our hips and behinds together. Still, I have forty years on David, so I soon retreated and went to rest in a back corner, at an empty table.

Marty joined me. Of all people. He plopped onto one of the padded conference chairs that flanked the round, cabaret-style table. He told a lame joke. I responded with a lame laugh. Marty sighed.

"I guess you think I'm the same jerk I was twenty-five years ago!" He slumped in the padded conference chair.

"Why Marty!" I exclaimed, roaring with delight. "I never knew you cared!"

Laura had kicked off her shoes long ago. She limped over in her stockinged feet and collapsed over the round, cabaret-style table, flinging her buxom upper body onto its surface and dropping her dark golden head into her arms. "I wish this was over. I'm tired. I'm sooo tired!"

A weary waitress who could not kick the shoes off her aching feet was clearing debris off surrounding tables. She looked at Laura with a mixture of envy and sadness.

"You've got a wonderful father." The waitress sighed.

How often had I heard that, and taken it for granted. Not knowing what to say to the waitress, I addressed Laura.

"Why don't you come up to my room and lie down?"

"If I lie down I'll never be able to get up." Laura moaned.

"So?" What a wonderful opportunity for Mum and me. "You can stay overnight with us. There are two queen-sized beds. You can take your pick choosing which one of us you'd like to cuddle with. We'd love to have you." For the moment, I blocked out my mother's disturbing symptoms.

"Nooo." Laura's timidity overrode her exhaustion. "That's OK. I'll just wait 'til it's over."

Having lost his dance partner, David took to collecting gum marbles and stuffing them into a party hat that looked like a Mad Hatter's hat. He shoved the oversized *chapeau* over his head and his eyes, without losing his marbles.

"David!" I called, as I stroked Laura's honey-gold hair. "Can you find me by following the sound of my voice?"

David extended his arms, staggered around the tables, most of which were empty, now, and zeroed in on his sister, Marty and me. Impressively, he removed his hat while managing to retain his marbles.

"Wait a minute!" David deposited the hat, its underside up, at our table, and raced across the hall to retrieve a party favour. It was an illuminated emerald hoop. Solemnly and ceremoniously David placed it on my head, like a crown. He sat at the table and studied me.

"You're an angel because you have a halo."

It was the witching hour; time for a Mad Hatter and a golden-haired *bat mitzvah* girl and an angel with an emerald halo, and even a poor little rich boy to emerge from their corner and say goodnight. As a sleepy waitress cleared the tables, we trudged out of the hall and into the hotel lobby. Marty joined his family in their top floor suite, while David and Laura descended the wide staircase, disappeared through a revolving door, entered their daddy's waiting car, and were swallowed up by the night. I stood alone in the lobby. Mum snuck up behind me.

"What is that thing on your head?! You're all lit up!"

"Oh!" I laughed. "It's a party favour. I'll take it off." I raised my arm, on the verge of doing so.

"No!" Mum protested. "Leave it on. You look gorgeous!"

I dropped my arm. Mum slipped her hand into mine.

"Our kids." Mum wrapped her arm around my waist. "Those are our kids! Why couldn't your father have lived to see them?" We seemed to miss Daddy more in the good moments, than in the difficult ones. In vain, Mum appealed to a deaf Universe.

"Why was he taken from me so soon?" She lowered her head onto my shoulder.

"I bet you never expected to see a granddaughter turn thirteen." I nestled my head on top of hers.

"Oh sweetheart." Mum buried her head further into the crook of my neck. Feeling safe in my arms, she allowed herself to reveal the hidden child who was denied a childhood. I stroked my mother's greying hair, as I had stroked my niece's golden hair. The light emanating from my halo illuminated its silver strands.

"Darling," my mother whispered, as if confessing a guilty secret, "I never expected to live long enough to see myself turn thirteen."

HITTING BELOW THE BIBLE BELT

Sioux City, Iowa –The spring of 2009

"Find me someone connected to the film, and find me someone connected to the story," the billionaire instructed his assistant, Cindy Lou. Cindy Lou ran an Internet search and came up with the name of one of the writers who was listed in the film's joint credits for screenwriting. Then she found Renia.

The Jewish philanthropist was the son of a Russian immigrant who, because he couldn't speak English, worked in Sioux City's stockyards hauling dead meat. Annually Joe Orshan sponsored an event he termed *Tolerance For A Week*, because he didn't want to alienate his Christian neighbours by calling it Holocaust Week. During this week singled out for Judeo-Christian brotherhood, Joe sponsored the screening of a Holocaust-related film. Several years earlier Renia served as historical consultant on the film *The Courageous Heart of Irena Sendler*, and since Joe chose this film for the coming event, a search was launched for Renia. She was located through Montreal's Holocaust Memorial Centre, where she worked as a volunteer guide. Then an invitation was issued to Renia and an escort of her choice to fly to Iowa for the event, all expenses paid. To accompany her, Renia chose the woman she deemed her memory keeper. Me. I was, am, and always will be Renia's daughter.

The invited writer flitted on the margins of Hollywood's film industry for years, and earned credit for co-writing one horror film. He was cut out of the screenwriting process on the film about Sendler when the producer brought an experienced writer on board. In retaliation, Lewis took his successor to arbitration at the Screenwriters Guild. As a result, the producer listed Lewis' name among the credits in order to avoid a lawsuit. When Mum asked, she was told that the man responsible for the screenplay was invited and then uninvited when he demanded more money than Orshan's organization was prepared to pay. In fact, the legitimate screenwriter wasn't approached at all. Cindy Lou hadn't done her homework. Orshan's organization would get what they paid for, and then some.

On the morning after our arrival in Iowa, Mum was escorted to a press conference with the screenwriter, who was not only introduced as a screenwriter, but as an historian, too. Inaccuracies in his comments disturbed her. Privately, she corrected him. The hack who dared to promote himself as an historian did not take kindly to what he perceived as an old woman's interference.

The same evening Lewis, Mum and I gathered in the lobby waiting for Orshan and his entourage. The private driver who met us at the Omaha airport pulled up in a stretch limousine. Orshan's entourage included a psychiatrist from Florida and a survivor of Auschwitz, now retired and residing in Florida. Both were flown in annually, and the Auschwitz survivor had become the poster child for these events. The camp survivor was a patient of the psychiatrist. They appeared to be almost a couple, except that the psychiatrist didn't hold the survivor's hand. Well, maybe he did, metaphorically.

We all climbed into the air-conditioned limousine, with its fully-equipped bar, for the two-minute ride to the Orpheum Theatre. Lewis ogled me. As he leered and suggestively waggled his head, his toupee slipped.

Before the screening, a gala dinner was held in the theatre's lobby. Mum and I were seated with the philanthropist at the table of honour. A special meal was prepared for him. The son of a man who had hauled cow carcasses in local stockyards was a vegan.

Orshan's second wife, who wasn't Jewish, was in attendance. Her name was Bonnie and in their country club, which was private and protected, the couple was known as Joe and Bo. Bo wore hair that didn't move, a mask of make-up, glittery shoes with spikes that verged on dangerous, and kept alkaline strips in her purse.

"We have five homes," Bo informed me. "We have a ranch here in Iowa, but our main house is across the border, in South Dakota, because the state is tax-free. Joe keeps an office in Toronto and wanted to buy a house there but I scotched that idea. 'Are you kidding?!' I told him. 'And run the risk of tripping over the homeless?!' So we bought a house in that suburb which sounds like Mississippi. As a Canadian, you probably know what I mean."

"Mississauga." I was starting to choke on my salad, and reached for a glass of water.

"Don't touch that!" Bo commanded. "Not yet." She reached into her purse and pulled out her alkaline strips. "The water is acidic. This will alkalinize it." Bo dunked a strip into my glass of water and then passed strips around the table, insisting her guests do the same. "Joe, honey, would you like me to alkalinize your water, too?"

"No, Baby. I like my water acidic." Joe winked at me and turned to the town rabbi, who was seated on his other side. "I'm an acidic Jew!"

Realizing that I had been lifted into the stratosphere of the stinking rich and wildly ridiculous, I adapted quickly.

"Do you have a private plane?' I attempted small talk with Joe.

"I used to, sweetie, but I gave it up. The upkeep on those things is expensive!" So there really is a limit to everything.

After dinner the guests were invited to adjourn to an adjoining lounge, where the local media interviewed Lewis.

135

Mum was agitated by the inaccuracies of his answers. Then the guests and the audience settled into the main hall of the theatre. The hall was packed. Thanks to the philanthropist, admission was free.

The film was powerful, and the audience sat hushed. Bo was deeply disturbed by one scene.

"When the baby is sedated and put into a box that's taken out of the Warsaw Ghetto, why did her parents put a silver spoon beside her? I know they engraved her name and birth date on the spoon, but silver is a metal, and metal contains toxins!"

After the screening of the film both Lewis and Mum were invited onstage in order to take questions from the audience. A local radio talk show host served as the evening's master of ceremonies. Mum and Lewis were positioned in front of a podium that held one microphone, and were expected to share it. Some questions were addressed to Lewis; some questions were addressed to Mum. Bizarrely, without warning, Lewis turned and left the stage. Mum stood alone. She grew confused. Assuming the Question and Answer period was over, she limped down the set of stairs placed in front of the stage, supported by her cane. Mum's cancer was in its third remission, but she had developed arthritis in one of her hips.

When Mum vacated the stage, just as suddenly as he vanished, Lewis reappeared. He bounded onto the platform, installed himself behind the podium, and held centre stage. Since questions were still being addressed to Mum, the master of ceremonies found himself running back and forth with his microphone, between Mum and members of the audience. Increasingly confused, she stood leaning on her cane, near the bottom of the stage. When Lewis was questioned, it was obvious to Mum and I that he didn't know the answers. To us, it was also obvious that the audience was even more ignorant than the screenwriter, and accepted his answers as fact. Promoting himself on the back of the legitimate writer and director of the film, Lewis invented answers. He couldn't be accused of lying, because he didn't know what the truth was. Mum's distress escalated as a Hollywood hack hijacked the Holocaust. When questions were addressed to Mum she appeared calm and her words were coherent and clear, but I noticed that she was angling the microphone away from her mouth. As a pioneer in Holocaust Education, Mum knew how to use a microphone.

In an attempt to rescue her, I signalled the master of ceremonies and he positioned his microphone beneath my lips.

"Mum. I have a question."

Mum looked dazed. She was disoriented and unable to decipher where my voice was coming from.

"Mummy, I'm here!" I shouted. The forthright declaration and the amplified sound of my voice re-focused my mother. "Mum!" I let the audience know – I let the screenwriter know – that this old woman wasn't alone. "When you and Bieta – who was the baby that was sedated and smuggled out of the Warsaw Ghetto in a box—" For the audience, I identified the Polish woman whom Mum considered her best friend. "When the two of you petitioned the Polish pope in your campaign to have Sendler nominated for the Nobel Peace Prize, what was his response?"

Mum snapped to attention. "He helped, of course!" Forcefully, Mum addressed the citizens of America's Heartland. "The pope pitched in and together we succeeded in having Sendler nominated. She didn't win the award. The year she was nominated, the Nobel Peace Prize went to the man who was then your vice-president, Al Gore."

The Midwestern audience was gobsmacked. It took the master of ceremonies a moment to retrieve his voice. Pensively, he spoke into his microphone.

"Does anyone else have any other questions – if you can top that!"

Alone in our room at the Holiday Inn, Mum was exceptionally quiet. I was at her feet, helping her out of her shoes and stockings. Mum gazed tenderly at me. "Payback time!" She batted her eyelashes. Without assistance Mum lifted off her dress, and then undid her bra. She had to drop its straps below her shoulders and twist the back to the front in order to undo the hooks. I watched sadly, remembering when she could easily wrap her arms around her back in order to undo a bra. Mum had grown stiffer, and her range of motion was increasingly limited.

I helped Mum into bed, removed the cane to a safe corner, and tucked her in. Then I got into my own bed on the other side of the nightstand, and shut the bedside lamp. I began drifting into sleep. Mum tossed and turned.

"Are you awake?" She asked, hopefully.

"Mmmmm," I muttered drowsily.

"I can't sleep."

"I know." I knew I wouldn't get much sleep on this night, either.

Wordlessly Mum hauled herself out of her bed, limped over to where I lay, climbed in with me, and curled into my waiting arms.

"Why did he do it?" Mum whimpered, feeling weakened and defeated by the evening's events.

"Who knows?" I sighed.

"Is that what the Americans call a 'Hollywood hack'?"

"That guy," I snapped, "is what the Americans call an asshole!"

138

"What a phoney." Mum pouted, like a petulant child. "Even his hair is fake!"

I stroked my mother's hair. It had recently grown back, after the latest round of chemo treatments. My mother's virgin hair was lovelier and even more luxuriant than before.

"Well, Mum, that phoney is going back to Hollywood tomorrow, and you're not. You've got the rest of the week to turn this around. Make the most of it."

My mother rolled over to remove the pressure off her hurting hip. She pressed her back against me. I wrapped my arms around her. In response, Mum latched onto my hands and held them in a tight and desperate grip.

The next day, speaking to a group of students at a Christian fundamentalist college Mum, still smarting from the debacle of the previous evening, allowed herself to unleash. Generally when lecturing to students in her capacity as a Holocaust educator, Mum gave sanitized versions of her victimization in wartime. Not this time. She did not spare the young people details of the horrors and atrocities she had witnessed and suffered when she was younger than they were. When asked by a fresh-faced girl if she drew comfort from religion Mum blasted, "No! I do not believe in God. If I did, I'd take him to court! When innocent men, women and children were ordered, at gunpoint, to strip naked and then shot into the pits they were forced to dig in order to create their common grave, the last thing they saw before being murdered was the inscription on the belts of the Germans – not the Nazis, which was a political party – but the Germans – and it read "God is with us". If God was with the Germans, then God is the devil!" The students were galvanized. One black student slumped glumly, in the back. Mum's eyes caught his, and held them. "You have a history of slavery and oppression in this country, too." The black student perked up. "You're not responsible for what your grandparents did." Fiercely, Mum eyeballed the white students. "But you must accept that they did it." The black student smirked. His classmates gasped. "Now remember me." My mother's medical prognosis cast a constant shadow. "When I'm gone, you will be my witnesses." The students leapt to their feet and rushed the stage, swamping the sick old woman in bear hugs, kisses and tears.

For the rest of the week, Mum lectured to electrified crowds in America's Bible Belt. At the end of her stay, the philanthropist offered her a thousand dollar honorarium. She refused to accept a personal cheque.

"I don't make money off the Holocaust. If you want to make a donation, you can send a cheque to the Association of Hidden Children in Poland. They are taking care of elderly Poles who rescued them during the war. A few of these rescuers are still alive."

Mum and I sat side by side in the back seat of the limousine chauffeuring us to the airport in Omaha. The large, thick windows were tinted. Like local celebrities who had ridden in this vehicle before us, we could look out, but no one could see in. Mum sat peacefully, satisfied with another mission accomplished. I gazed at my mother's profile, which had once been chiselled, and now was beginning to sag. A woman who survived three wartime invasions and the infamous Warsaw Ghetto was slowly and inexorably being destroyed by the negligence of a sloppy Jewish doctor. After repeatedly reporting symptoms and repeatedly being dismissed, Mum was belatedly diagnosed with a slow-growing, easy-to-catch cancer. To me, my mother's final victimization was beyond tragic; it was absurd. To avoid becoming engulfed by grief, I had trained myself not to look too far ahead.

I lifted my mother's wrinkled and liver-spotted hand, pressed it to my cheek, and kissed it. Then I followed her gaze to the view of the foothills and cornfields and cottonwood trees whizzing past. For the moment, Death could wait.

SORRY FOR YOUR LOSS

Mississauga, Ontario – The early winter of 2013

My mother Renia was finally dead. For a decade following her cancer, diagnosis she clung tenaciously to life in order not to leave me. I became Mum's protector and caregiver. Mum knew she was my life. We lived for each other. Now she was gone, and I wished I could go.

"Pack a bag and be ready to leave as soon as you can," Mark instructed. Mark had taken a leave of absence from his post as a doctor in Ontario and moved into our mother's apartment in Montreal in order to help fulfil her wish to die at home.

Though she lived and died in Montreal, Mum asked to be buried in Ontario. Mark was transplanted there, and her grandchildren were rooted there. Mum also instructed that Daddy's remains be transferred and laid beside her.

I packed for a week's stay. Though Mum had insisted there be no *shiva*, nor even a chapel service, my birthday was in a week. As conditioned as I am to solitary confinement, under the circumstances I was not prepared to spend my upcoming birthday alone. Still, I knew what to expect. I also knew what not to expect.

Mark and I hit the road. Our mother's corpse was transported in a separate vehicle. Darkness dropped like a final curtain. There was no snow on the highway, and no moon in the sky. We hadn't placed an obituary, but I sent a group e-mail to several people, and word-of-mouth did the rest. Bad news travels fast, so *They* say, and it turns out *They* are right. Disembodied voices echoed in the sealed chamber of Mark's SUV, as condolence calls came in from around the globe.

Approaching midnight, we approached Mark's Mississauga home. The lights were on. The dogs perked up. David was away

142

at university. Vivian was in Australia. Laura, who attended a nearby art college, was at home. Erin opened the front door.

"Daddy's home!" Laura sprang at Mark. So did the two dogs, both the smart dog, and the dumb one. I stood in the doorway like a piece of unwanted luggage.

"I'm going for a walk," I declared. Then I turned and marched out into the cold, crisp air. After the six-hour drive, walking was a welcome relief.

The residential streets were wide and empty. The houses were dark, and seemed asleep. The bare maple branches and leafy evergreens stood mute. I did not leave the street Mark lived on yet I grew disoriented, and couldn't find my way back. The air that at first felt bracing was turning frigid. Unlike most people these days, I am not glued to a mobile phone. "Find me," I projected a telepathic message to my brother. "Come out and find me!"

Obligingly, a hulking SUV, like an army tank, lumbered down the silent road. I ran into the middle of the road and waved.

"You were taking too long." Mark masked his nervousness.

"I know." I didn't hide my anxiety. "I couldn't find my way back. I was hoping you'd figure it out, and find me."

When we walked through Mark's door I almost commanded, "Get me drunk. Give me a drink."

"Pick your poison." Mark led me to his makeshift bar. Perusing the selection, I honed in on a fat-bottomed bottle of *Courvoisier*.

"That was Daddy's favourite drink," I remembered, out loud. "I'll have it."

Mark measured out a modest amount of the amber-coloured liquid, poured it into a snifter, and handed it to me. I knew to swirl the snifter in circular motions, since I've seen it done in movies.

"Ahh, *quel bouquet!*" I mimicked my dad.

Because I rarely drink, the alcohol took quick effect. The sensation of burnt orange on my tongue compelled me to slow down and calm down. The image of my mother's slack-jawed and discoloured visage, as it looked at the end, was pressing itself upon me. The bursts of toffee and chocolate and the slight alcohol sting drew me below the surface of the unbearable present, and would soon lull me into sleep.

"Watch the stairs," Mark cautioned, as I headed to the basement bedroom vacated by Vivian. In the basement, in the den, I sat nursing the last sips of cognac. A twenty-year-old photograph of Mum flashed from a corner of the wall. It gazed kindly upon me, and I took myself to bed.

The next morning I sat in Mark's living room, writing Mum's eulogy. Mark and Laurie were at the funeral home, making arrangements. Laurie had also relocated to Ontario. When the men returned, the bargaining began.

"There are so many people who want to pay their respects to Mum that it would be disrespectful not to let them," Mark decided.

"But Mum didn't want any of that fuss. She called it a circus of hypocrisy."

"I spoke to Rabbi Danny," Mark barrelled on. "We don't have to hold a week-long shiva. Rabbi Danny says we could hold a three-day memorial service, or keep it to one evening. I understand what Mum wanted, but you know she was a modest person and didn't realize the impact she had. The idea is to respect her wishes while considering the feelings of those who loved her and want to honour her."

Mark could charm the birds out of the trees – when he wanted to shoot the birds. I acquiesced. "OK. But only one evening!"

I had given my hand. Now my arm would be sawed off.

"We'll have to be prepared to feed all the people who are bound to show up." Mark shifted into Gracious Host mode. "What kind of food can we order that you would be able to eat?" I am as sensitive to food as I am to everything else.

"Oh you don't need to do that!" Erin was moving in and out of the kitchen. Now she stood stock still in the hallway, barking at Mark. "Really! You don't prepare special food just for one person!"

Mark said nothing. Neither did Laurie. I know my sister-in-law, and I was prepared. At least, I thought I was prepared. "As a matter of fact, I was going to ask Mark to drive me to a supermarket tomorrow, so I can get provisions for myself."

"Oh you don't need to burden Mark any further! He has more than enough to do. Laura can drive you." It didn't take long for Erin to let me know where I stood.

I returned to composing our mother's eulogy. When I felt it was presentable, I read it to Mark and Laurie. They deemed my eulogy acceptable, but warned, "When we're at the cemetery, don't improvise!" Laurie had also written a eulogy, which he planned to read first. Neither Mark nor I thought of checking it. I took it on faith that whatever Laurie wrote would be acceptable.

The following day, without his wife's permission, Mark took me to the supermarket.

The next morning I walked into the kitchen to find Marty seated at the table. He had flown in from Zurich. He was on business there, with the intention and ticket to take him to his newly acquired condo in the Bahamas. His wife Leslie would join him. It took Marty twelve hours to fly from Europe instead of the standard six because he chose to fly to Florida first, in order to save half the fare on the ticket.

En route on this hastily rescheduled flight, *Swissair* lost his luggage.

Marty sat at the kitchen table recounting his travails.

"The Swiss lost my luggage! Imagine! The Swiss?!" I listened, without sympathy. Marty became aware of my presence. Quickly he pulled on the face he keeps for such occasions, rose from the table, and strode over to me.

"Sorry for your loss." Marty's tone was inorganically lugubrious and sounded silly.

I thrust out my arm in a gesture of self-protection.

"Nothing!" I burst. "There is nothing to say!" Marty backed off. Erin darted a dirty look in my direction. Laura looked perplexed.

David, my brother's youngest child, came in from university. With her children, Leslie drove in from Montreal. From around the world tributes poured in for the war orphan who had vowed to give her life meaning, and succeeded.

The day of the funeral was the first day of December. The atmosphere was suitably gloomy, and the date oddly appropriate. As a child, I loved the month into which I was born. The fresh snow and festive lights transformed my world into a fairyland. Due at Christmas, I was so eager to meet my mother that I emerged early, on St. Nicholas Day. As a child I imagined myself Santa's present to my parents and liked to believe the city I lived in, which kept Christmas well, was celebrating my birthday all month long. Now, in a bleak and windswept field, under a dull and leaden sky, I would escort out of the world the woman who brought me into it.

Leslie strode into view, along a grey and frozen path. She was draped in an ankle-length coat of black fake fur, and her honey-coloured hair was cupped in a large white beret. Her image was reminiscent of a bird of prey.

"Noela!" Leslie prided herself on her social grace. "Look! I'm wearing a brooch your mother gave me! Isn't it lovely?"

My stare was blank. Leslie backtracked. "I'm not trying to take anything away from you!" Why should she? Leslie already had it. My mother was an extremely generous woman, and considered Leslie part of the family. Mum was also pragmatic. She gave Leslie her best dinnerware set, since Leslie has the mansion and means to entertain, and I don't.

"Would you like to come to my house for dinner on Thursday evening, for your birthday?" Leslie offered charitably.

I didn't bother to remind Leslie that my birthday was not on Thursday, but on Friday. Leslie knew it. Leslie didn't mention that, on my birthday, she and Marty would be flying to the Bahamas.

"I'm not going back to Montreal until after the sixth." It was my way of letting Leslie know what I thought of her charity.

"Oh! Well!" Leslie was relieved. "It's good to know you'll be staying here with family, but I wanted you to know you were invited. It's going to be tough on you when you get back. You should take up meditation. You can get a free mantra on the internet." Leslie was considerate of my financial constraints.

"Nice coat," I mumbled, in lieu of something genuine to say.

"You like it? I got it at *Winner's*." In full view of my mother's coffin, Leslie twirled and modelled her latest acquisition. "It cost nothing!"

"How much is nothing?"

"A hundred and ninety-nine ninety five!"

Some bargain. For me, that is plenty of nothing.

The mourners gathered at the gravesite. Rabbi Danny made the standard remarks I assume he makes on these occasions.

147

Then Laurie, sounding more like a rabbi than the rabbi, delivered his eulogy. Laurie's retelling of a wartime anecdote he heard from Mum was historically impossible and impossibly sanitized. He even got her age wrong. The coffin containing my dead mother was still resting on the surface of the earth. "Oh Mum." I was as appalled as she would be, and as silent as she had become. "We haven't buried you yet, and they're already getting your story wrong."

When Laurie was mercifully done, I delivered my eulogy. It was short, concise, and half of it was a tribute to what I perceived as the quiet heroism of my brother.

"Our Mother Courage waged an epic battle with cancer. It became obvious that she was going to lose, yet she submitted to the torturous surgeries and treatments in exchange for time. Our mother loved us fiercely and equally, but I am the one she feared for... During the last weeks of Mum's life Mark served as doctor, nurse, orderly, waiter, companion, counsellor and spiritual healer. Mark cocooned our mother in a sanctuary of security and serenity. As she gazed adoringly at Mark, and at me, Mum was able to say, "I lost only the battle, sweetheart. The war, I won.""

As Mark relived our mother's final days through my words, he broke down and wept. The colleagues, both doctors and nurses, who covered for him during his absence, were visibly moved.

Mum's coffin was lowered into a gaping hole dug in the nearly frozen ground, and those who chose took turns lifting the communal shovel and tossed token amounts of earth into the open grave.

"I lost six hundred dollars!" Laurie wailed.

"What?" After the funeral, those considered part of the

family gathered in Mark's home, except for Marty, who went shopping to replace the clothes he needed for his break in the Bahamas.

"I lost six hundred dollars!" Laurie reiterated. "I had to cancel my trip to New York this weekend and I couldn't get the money back on the flight! I was going to take the kids to see a Broadway show! The travel insurance agent told me I could only collect money because of death if the death was the death of a parent. 'But she was like a mother to me!' I told the guy. 'She was better than my mother!' But he was brutal. He wouldn't reimburse me. I lost six hundred dollars!"

"Sorry for you loss," I mumbled, and escaped into the basement.

Hiding in the basement, I fell into a deep sleep. Perched at the edge of Vivian's bunk bed, a diaphanous sprite shape-shifted into a dream.

"At funerals, you bury one," the spirit reminded me. "At weddings, you bury two!"

"Not at this funeral, Dad," I contradicted Daddy's spirit. "At this funeral, along with Mum, I am being buried alive."

"To be buried alive is to be like a planted seed. From a planted seed, a healthy thing can grow," the spirit prophesied.

"You have to get up and come upstairs for the memorial service!" Laurie had found me and was shaking me awake.

The caterer had delivered, and a buffet was set in the dining room. A separate order was placed for Marty and Leslie's brood, since all three of their children have the lethal nut allergy. Leslie drove to the local *Chalet Bar-B-Q* to pick up her children's dinner, only to discover that the restaurant got the order wrong. Dinner for her children would have to be reordered and it would take another hour to prepare, so the ceremony was delayed. Erin insisted that the mourners wait, out of respect for her friends and their children.

Marty burst through the door. "They found my luggage! I just spent a fortune replacing my wardrobe and now the airline found my luggage!"

"Sorry for your loss," I mused drowsily.

When the revised food order finally arrived, Erin allowed the memorial service to begin. Marty's eighteen-year-old son grinned at me.

"Hi! How are ya?"

I glared at him. "Are you serious?"

Jimmy did a double take. "Oh!" He quickly recalibrated, and connected the dots. "Oh ya! Mark's sister!" Smart boy. "Sorry for your loss!" Just as quickly, Jimmy sprinted away. A very smart boy.

Pretty, blonde Bradley glided into view. He had inherited his mother's good looks and social grace. Bradley was studying for a degree in economics, and worked part-time as a model. His father was so proud of this that he showed off eight-by-ten glossy photographs of his sneering and half-nude child to anyone who would sit still long enough to look at them. Bradley was a fine specimen promoting a good example of physical fitness. So his mother said.

"Hi! How are ya!" Bradley parroted his younger brother.

Again, I glared. "You've got to be kidding."

Like his brother, Bradley snapped to attention and remembered his father's training. "Oh! Oh ya! Sorry for your loss!"

Lana, the boys' sister, must have been on the premises, too. Wherever she was, she steered clear of me.

My niece Laura was sincerely saddened by her grandmother's death. For comfort, she surrounded herself with a coterie of classmates. They decorated the hallways and draped themselves over the furniture while texting each other, hunched over their smart phones like rodents scrolling on treadmills.

"Sorry!" Jimmy bellowed, to a disembodied voice across the universe. Somewhere in the Australian Outback, Vivian was on the other end of an exceptionally intelligent and expensive phone.

"For what?!" Vivian bellowed back. Jimmy hadn't done anything.

"For your loss! Jimmy wailed.

"Oh!" It took Vivian more than a New York minute to decipher what was going on in Canada. "Oh, thaaaat!"

Jimmy just couldn't get it right. I was starting to feel sorry for Marty's boy.

Rabbi Danny called the gathering to order. As the chief mourners, Mark and I were called to stand behind him. Without being summoned, David stepped up and stood by his dad. The prayers began. Mark wept. I placed a hand on one side of my brother's back, and David placed a hand on the other side. Tentatively I stretched out my hand, and David accepted it. Aunt and nephew stood silently with joined hands, supporting the man who had lost his mother.

The prayers ended. I relinquished my nephew's hand, and let go of my brother.

"You think it's hard now? Wait until you get home! It's gonna hit you like a ton of bricks! This is nothing! When you get home you'll sink so low you won't know where bottom is!" Marilyn grinned like a chipmunk with nuts between its teeth. Supposedly she had come to pay her respects to the bereaved.

"This isn't helpful," I said, stating the obvious.

"Oh it's going to get even harder!" Marilyn, older than I and still in possession of a full set of parents, was in full verbal flight.

"Marilyn," I warned. "I just said this isn't helpful."

"Pain! Oh the paaaain!" Marilyn's monologue grew

orgasmic. "Now you're surrounded by people who comfort you, but when you go home and find yourself alone, you'll find out what pain really is!" Marilyn rhapsodized.

"Then I'm lucky I've got no more parents left to lose."

Marilyn blinked. I walked away. Denied the pleasure of tormenting an orphan, Marilyn set her sights on Marty. "You're cute!" The married Marilyn winked, lasciviously smacking her lips.

Unless an airline lost his luggage, Marty was imperturbable. Except for now. Now he was unnerved. Marty ran to Mark for protection. "That old lady's got the hots for me!"

I hung on and held out in anticipation of my nightly dose of cognac. It was the only thing I looked forward to. After the guests left I headed to Mark's makeshift bar. The fat-bottomed bottle wasn't there.

"Mark, where's the cognac? I can't find it."

"It should be there." My brother came over to help me look. Every other liquor bottle was in its place, but the cognac had mysteriously disappeared.

"Erin may have tossed it when she was getting the room ready for the guests." Mark searched for a rationale and too quickly found it. "She must've thought it was empty."

Erin, who was hovering nearby, said nothing. Neither did I. I descended the stairs to the basement and collapsed onto Vivian's bed. The next morning I was unable to leave it. Long angry welts dug into the surface of my torso. My skin appeared as if it had been lashed with a whip.

"It hurts to breathe," I managed to gasp, as Mark looked in, at the doorway.

"Would you like me to get you anti-histamines?" Like most of his colleagues, Mark is prepared to treat symptoms while ignoring their cause.

"No. I've had hives before. It will pass."

At my request, Mark bought another bottle of cognac, which I kept hidden until I got home. I hid my non-perishable food items too, in case the black hole in Mark's bar extended to Erin's kitchen. Erin didn't find my food, but the dumb dog did. As dumb as he was, he was still a dog. He followed his nose, leapt into my shopping trolley, toppled the trolley and its contents, and ran with the sugar-free macaroons.

"Is Tipperary alright? What did you put in there?" For the first time, Erin demonstrated real emotion. Her two dogs were male dogs. The smart dog was named for a female character in the Harry Potter children's book series, and the dumb dog was named for a city in Ireland.

"I hope you didn't have chocolate in your bag." Erin was genuinely alarmed. "It could kill him!" She was truly in fear for her dog's life.

"No." I was itchy, hungry and exhausted. Feebly, I attempted to defend myself. "There was no chocolate in the macaroons."

"We would've had to take Tipperary to the hospital!" Erin hurled at the would-be dog killer in her midst. "Thank god!" It was a lucky dog that got to live with Erin.

Tipperary ate my chocolate and nothing happened to him," muttered Laura, from behind her laptop. Laura and her laptop were inseparable. Luckily for Laura, her mother didn't hear her.

Mark took the week off from work. In the mornings he went to synagogue to say prayers for our mother; in the afternoons he walked his dogs, and me. The sedate older dog, Huffelpuff, dragged himself along the sidewalk. He was not only an older dog; he had become an old dog. Tipperary would go berserk and spin in circles each time a car passed. Fortunately, the streets we walked don't see heavy traffic.

Having returned to university, David called on my birthday. Vivian did not. Vivian called the next day.

"I wasn't there! I wasn't there! I didn't tell anybody about it. I wasn't there!" Ten days after her grandmother's death, the news was sinking in.

"What are you talking about, sweetheart?" Mark's tone turned tender.

"I didn't tell anybody here. I didn't tell anybody here about Grandma!"

"Sweetheart, you have nothing to feel guilty about."

Hearing this conversation over the speakerphone, I swallowed my visceral response, and continued packing.

"You came with us to visit grandma when we first – knew what was happening." Mark choked on his euphemism. "Grandma was an intrepid traveller, and so are you."

"I'm carrying on the family tradition!" Vivian sniffled.

"That's right. Your grandmother was proud of you. She would be happy that you're having a chance to see the world."

"I'm traveling for Grandma!" Vivian was turning into her own cheerleader.

"Now you go out and have a wonderful day."

Vivian had her daddy's blessing. "Onward and upward!" Vivian roared, like a sports coach. "OK mates!" Having picked up the vernacular, Vivian called to her Aussie companions. "I'm on my way!"

I lugged my full bag and lifted my empty shopping trolley into the back of my brother's SUV. Mark was driving me back to Montreal.

The couple Mark considered family came through for him. Since it would be too much to expect their bereaved friend to drive back and forth to Mississauga in one day, and it would be too cruel to leave him alone overnight in his dead mother's empty apartment, Marty and Leslie

154

gave him a spare key to their suburban mansion. It entered no one's mind that my brother might've stayed with me.

Mark was on his way back to Mississauga. It was my first evening alone in the world. I cobbled together a meal from leftovers in my fridge. I was chopping up half a head of Savoy cabbage. As I chopped, I nibbled. I needed to bite into something. The ridges of a cabbage leaf stuck in my throat. There was no bread in the house, with which to push down the leaf. Liquid didn't work. The cabbage leaf wouldn't dislodge. My jaw and throat muscles had shut down. I couldn't swallow anymore. I began to choke. There was no point calling 911, because I wasn't able to communicate. The logical step would've been to run to a neighbour for help and point to my throat, but I chose not to. My eyes dilated and began to tear. Whistling sounds emerged from my tortured throat. Slowly strangling, I sank to my knees. As much as I wanted to die, this was really painful. In the back of my cramping skull I heard a woman's voice command, "Decide." I was on my knees and doubled over. Louder, fiercely insistent, the voice dictated, "Decide!" Then the voice decided for me. There was a cosmic smack on the back of my lungs, like a baby being brought to life, and the ragged piece of cabbage leaf flew, like a projectile, out of my mouth.

MOVING THE FURNITURE

Christmas Time, 2013 and early January, 2014

"Silent Night, Holy Night, all is calm, all is bright…" Over CBC Radio, a choir carolled. Outside my mother's windows, wind howled and a blizzard raged. Disoriented, I shuffled through her disordered apartment. Grief, the textbooks called it. Bereavement, the textbooks added. Mark was paying the rent on Mum's apartment and gave me three weeks to sort through her possessions before coming in to dispose of the surplus. He scheduled three days for the purging process. I warned him that three days wouldn't be enough.

"Oh I bet I could do it in one day! You just put stickers on what you want to take and we'll do the rest." Mark blasted, like a cold wind. More and more he disregarded and overrode my concerns. With Erin, Mark charged into Mum's apartment two days after Christmas. They had spent Christmas with her parents. Christmas was their holiday, after all. Mark was devoted to his in-laws.

Once Mark was in town, Marty resurfaced. Mark's family and Marty's family considered themselves one big happy family.

Ignoring the detailed notes I e-mailed to him, Mark tore through Mum's apartment, tossing items I cautioned him to leave and flinging aside items I hadn't time to sort through and make decisions on. When I pleaded with him to slow down he barked, "I don't have a lot of time and you can't do this by yourself. Don't be so materialistic!" In the presence of Marty and Erin, my brother delivered the coup de grace. "Anyway, you had three weeks!" Once more, I was cowed into silence.

Cheerfully, Marty purged areas of the apartment assigned to him. He was focused and efficient, yet not too rushed to miss details. How helpful it would have been if he had come in to assist when I was alone.

Triumphantly Erin sat on the hide-a-bed where Mum lay after chemotherapy treatments, a laptop on her lap, scrutinizing her dead mother-in-law's furniture and making notes on what she might like to keep and what might be given away. Erin gave to charity. With strangers, Erin was generous.

"I'm taking the curio case. It will fit into a corner of my living room." I informed Mark.

"You must take your mother's bookcase." Astonishingly, my sister-in-law spoke directly to me. She was also casting a covetous eye on the crystal-filled curio case.

"I've got a bookcase. I don't have room for two."

"You can put one bookcase into your kitchen," Erin insisted, as she fixated on the gleaming crystals in the glass and redwood case. This time I was the one who ignored Erin.

"What about the chandelier?" I reminded Mark. "I sent you an e-mail about that." Mum had been adamant. Repeatedly she reminded me, "The chandelier was a gift from Daddy. Don't let it go. It belongs in the family."

Mark was bleary-eyed. For hours he'd been blindly discarding reminders of the past. "We've decided not to take it down."

We? Surely it was only the dead woman's direct descendants who had the right to decide the fate of her effects.

"Marty says it's worthless."

Marty was at the door, pulling on his parka.

As exhausted as I was, I snapped to attention. "But Mum said it was valuable!"

"Well Mum was wrong!" Mark shot back.

"Oh men are always lying to their wives about how

much they spend on gifts for them." Marty was stepping into his designer boots, now. Erin rolled her eyes and donned her quilt-lined coat.

This was one decision I was determined to defy. While still having access to her apartment, I discreetly arranged for the removal and safekeeping of Daddy's gift to Mum.

On this first day of the apartment purge, after the trio left I remained alone in Mum's apartment, sorting through the books in her personal library and laying clothes on an open ironing board that I thought might prove suitable for and attractive to my heavy-set niece Laura.

Though Mum's apartment wasn't fully dismantled, on the last day of the purge Mark, Erin and Marty left early. They were determined to respect Leslie's dinnertime. Freezing rain rendered the roads treacherous, and before darkness fell they aimed to reach Marty's Laurentian Hills house. I watched them leave, and then called Leslie.

"Is it possible? Everyone is going to spend New Year's up north, except me?"

"But my dear!" Leslie cooed. "There will be a lot of children in the house. It will be noisy. You've been through a trying time. You need rest."

"Let me get this straight." I was trying to process what I had just heard. "It's almost New Year's Eve, Mum's been dead a month, everyone is going to be together, and I am going to be alone?"

The answer was in the question. The moment of abandonment had come. I was shocked, but not surprised. Still, I couldn't envision how grotesque my situation was going to become.

"I'm still up north in the country." Marty spent most weekends at his country house. It was respite from his suburban mansion.

"If you have nothing better to do, would you go to your mother's apartment and sit there until the charity workers come." From Marty, this was not a request; it was an order.

"No!" I exploded, into the telephone receiver.

"What?!" Marty wasn't used to being refused. Certainly not by me.

"I told Mark I require half an hour's notice from the time the workers call to say they're coming. These arrangements were made between you and Mark. I wasn't consulted. I'm never consulted. I'm only notified after the fact. He gave you a copy of Mum's keys. If you're not prepared to keep your word to my brother, don't expect me to cover for you," I snapped. "I've spent weeks alone in my mother's apartment, sorting through her stuff. I'm not going to spend another afternoon there just to do your waiting for you!"

"OK! OK!" Marty was taken aback. Generally I was meek and easy to handle. Why was I suddenly being unpleasant?

I hung up on Marty. Five minutes later, he called back. "They just called! They're on their way! They say they'll be in your mother's apartment in ten minutes!" Marty sounded panicked. "What should I do?!"

This was a switch. I had never known Marty to ask for advice; only to give it.

"That's your problem. The workers can wait, or they can leave. I don't have a car, and I certainly don't have wings. I said I require half an hour's notice. No more, but no less, either."

I hung up, got dressed, and attached spikes to my boots, preparing to walk on thin and black ice as well as the kind lurking in wait to trip up pedestrians under patches of innocent-looking snow. Then I marched out my door, into a bitter new year. Upon reaching Mum's apartment I wasn't surprised to find the door open and Marty already on the premises, directing and instructing the charity workers to move out furniture meant for me. There must be wings attached to his Land Rover, I thought. How did he get here so fast?

"That is supposed to come to me." I indicated a large-ticket item. "Leave it there." I instructed the workers, and warned Marty.

"I knew that." Marty admitted more than he meant to. Then he continued issuing orders. There were two charity workers; an older man, and a young one. The young man was the driver of the van. The role of the older man was unclear. Marty ordered the older man to take the dining room table sitting under the hole in the ceiling that had, until recently, held the chandelier Daddy gave to Mum.

"I don't want the table," the older man whined. "It's old."

I flinched. Marty is a businessman. Oblivious to my growing agitation, he moved into flea market mode.

"You can't take chairs without taking a table! When poor immigrants come from another country they will need a table to eat from, along with the chairs! You don't expect them to eat food off their laps, do you? They are going to need a table! You can't take the chairs without taking the table. And this is a Louis XV table!"

This was news to me. As for the charity worker, he didn't care which Louis the table belonged to. He came clean, blurting, "I'm seventy years old! That table is heavy!"

"Sir," I interjected. "You are under no obligation to take anything. I can call the Salvation Army."

Marty darted me a dirty look. Then he hissed and flayed out his hand in my direction, as if swatting at a pesky fly. In my mind, I was hearing Mum. *Don't you dare hold an*

160

estate sale, she had warned. *If you try to sell my stuff after I'm gone I'll come back and haunt you!* My feisty mama was only half-kidding. *My things are to be given away to people who can benefit from them. I don't want strangers coming into my apartment and pawing over my stuff!* I now spoke for the woman who could no longer speak for herself.

"I will not beg anyone to take my mother's furniture," I stated firmly to Marty. Then I reassured the charity worker. "Sir, you don't have to take a thing."

Marty's response was to dismiss me. "Leave!" He exploded, flinging out his arm towards Mum's open door. When I refused to obey his latest order Marty lunged at me, placed his palms forcefully upon my forearms, backed me to the edge of the apartment, and then shoved and pushed me out the door. Retrieving a handkerchief from his pocket and wiping his hands on it, Marty turned and returned his attention to the charity workers, derisively flapping an arm in my direction.

"Don't listen to her. I'm doing this for her brother."

The charity workers stared at Marty, seemingly paralysed. In the hallway, outside the door, I stood trembling. I found my voice, and discovered that it could roar.

"YOU get out!"

Marty and the charity workers, startled by the disruption, turned to the electrified vision roaring from beyond the door.

"This is my dead mother's house and this is my dead mother's stuff!" I vibrated, like a hot wire. "All of you! Everybody! Get out! Out! Out!"

The charity workers took off so quickly that they seemed to leave skid marks.

Marty couldn't fathom this turn of events. I had always been easy to control. A few verbal slaps were enough to keep me in place. Why was I asserting myself now?

161

"If I leave," Marty threatened, like a rejected lover, "I'll never come back!"

"GO!" I cried.

Was I serious? Marty was beginning to wonder. After all the help he and Leslie had extended to my family, this is how I repaid it. Marty wasn't going to countenance ingratitude. His next threat was savage and lethal.

"I'll have Mark take charge of you!"

The attacker and his target stood eyeball to eyeball. I knew what Marty meant. A decade spent as an unpaid caregiver ruined my economic earning power. I would be financially dependent on Mum's estate, which had been left to me. Mark was named executor of the estate and to my horror, Marty had been legally appointed second-in-command. Though Mum died loved and honoured, she didn't die rich. Marty believed he owned Mark. I knew that he did. I didn't doubt he would make good on his threat and my show of resistance would be punished. Softly, sadly and wearily I responded, "Get out, anyway."

Now Marty really was nonplussed. He had always been able to manipulate underlings by wielding money as a weapon. Though temporarily trumped, Marty still had the presence of mind to keep a promise he made to his wife. On his way out, he grabbed two needlepoint-cushioned chairs Leslie cast her eye on while visiting my dying mother. As Marty lifted them, the chairs' cushions dropped out of their frames. He stooped down to pick up the cushions and punched them back into their frames before waddling off, a chair under each arm, down the long corridor that led to the elevator. I retreated into the apartment, slammed the door and collapsed onto the closed hide-a-bed.

It was from the seat of this hide-a-bed that Mum reached out her arms to me as I entered the apartment each evening. Despite her increasing weakness, Mum's smile was wide and warm. "Here you are! Gimme a hug!" It was from there that Mum reclined in my arms, clasped my hands and gazed into my face like an adoring child. It was from this opened hide-a-bed that Mum rolled onto the carpeted floor in a drug-induced faint. Now I sat alone on the closed hide-a-bed, clasping my head and wrapping myself into my arms as I sobbed, screamed, and wept.

I was in my own bed. It was three o'clock in the morning. That's when the burning began. My face grew hot and pressure built in my head. I had never before experienced such symptoms. "If I'm going to have a stroke," I prayed, to no one and nothing in particular, "make it a massive one. Don't leave me here crippled."

"You're not getting out of the world so fast." Daddy's phantom honed in. Of course it did.

"I want to. As long as Mum was here I was still useful to the family. Now that she's with you, my purpose has been served."

I thought of the prescription for sleeping pills I was given, but hadn't filled. I was fed up with the tyranny of family. It was time to go.

"You're staying put." The tone of Daddy's phantom turned sharp.

"Daddy," I pleaded. "It's unbearable. Even worse, it's not worth it. I want out."

"Not you, not anyone is getting out of the world alive. But not yet. I put you there and left you to follow in *mein* footsteps and go further than me. You're a part of me. The best part. I always said you was a gift. *Mein* Noela, born on Santa Clauses Day. So brave. So strong. But maybe you think you were dropped down the wrong chimney?"

Was I delirious, or did I see Daddy's phantom wink?

" 'Vot is giving light must put up with burning.' " Daddy's

163

phantom paraphrased. Then it turned philosophical. "Every generation builds on top of the generation that was running around before."

"My generation didn't do better. We just had it easier because there was no war on."

The form of Daddy's phantom perched on the edge of my bed. Now he wasn't narrating a bedtime story. Now he was listening.

"I avoided marriage because I thought being married meant being victimized by in-laws. I saw what your sister did to Mum and swore that would never happen to me. But I was wrong. I didn't have to get married in order to be victimized by an in-law – it was enough for Mark to marry." My parents were dead, and I was defeated. "A lot would've been different if you had lived longer." I was angry with Daddy for dying too soon.

"*Mein* son lost me too early, I know." The phantom heaved a heavy-hearted sigh. "They took me away to The Other Side before he was even finished with school. He put Marty in my place. It wasn't a healthy thing to do. So yesterday you corrected your brother's mistake. But you were gentle with Louis XV." The mischievous gleam I remembered in Daddy's eyes during Daddy's lifetime now sparked from his phantom. "This king was lucky he got to leave by the door. If I still had *mein* fists he would be flying out the window, together with his chairs!" The phantom wiped his transparent palms with a gesture that signified Good Riddance, in the same manner that Marty had wiped his opaque palms.

"Aw Daddy." My head felt like it was on fire. Through the flames, despair broke through. "Take me with you. I don't want to be brave and strong. I want to be lucky. Why can't I be lucky? Why can't I be loved?"

The icy fingers of Daddy's phantom reached out to cool

164

and soothe my inflamed head. "If you give life another chance, it will bring you better people. New and improved. That's why you shouldn't leave it. And you have the memory of being loved. That will see you through everything."

As I curled into a foetal position, two shapes that were more than shadows and less than forms hovered over my bed while I cried brokenheartedly to a bare concrete wall.

THE DOLL LADY OF WISCONSIN

Superior, Wisconsin – The autumn of 2015

I was in Minnesota. I arrived in Duluth's shiny and tiny airport on a glowing October afternoon. As I waited for my suitcase at the luggage carrousel I spotted an old woman wearing blue jeans, with blades of white hair poking out of a white beret. She was staring at me. I picked up my suitcase and walked past her. The woman followed me. It was Imelda. She had been inaccurate in her description of herself, but I had described myself accurately enough to be recognized.

When I realized who this woman was, I threw my arms around her. Finally, I was meeting The Doll Lady of Wisconsin.

On the first anniversary of my mother's passing, a letter was forwarded by Montreal's Holocaust Memorial Centre. A woman in Wisconsin was writing a book and looking for my mother to provide her with background information. Enclosed were photographs of my mother, taken in her home over twenty years before.

Immediately I called the woman in Wisconsin. She told me she was a retired Health Educator. Indeed, she told me she had a Masters' degree in Health Education. She lived in a small town with the provocative name of Superior, because it was situated on Lake Superior. She said she had attended a conference in Cornwall, Ontario in the early 1990s and then took a side trip to Montreal on a Sunday afternoon, ending up on a tour of the Holocaust Centre.

The health educator's hobby was making dolls and giving them to people who struck her fancy. On her trip to Canada, in her suitcase she carried one of her homemade dolls. The woman in Wisconsin said that when my mother, who worked as a volunteer guide, took her on a tour of the Centre's museum, she knew the doll she was traveling with belonged to Mum.

According to this woman, the day after the tour she contacted the Centre, hoping to connect with my mother. Mum was notified, and she welcomed The Doll Lady into her home.

I remembered the doll and knew its story, though I had never met its creator. After first speaking with Imelda Dickinson, who I came to think of as The Doll Lady, I was annotating documents in my mother's hard drive when I stumbled upon her less dramatic version of events. In a document titled VICTIMIZED AGAIN? Mum wrote, *"After trauma people need time to recover and mourn. This is one reason why it's taken so much time for us to go public with our pain… In 1978 I journeyed with my children to Poland – into my past – it became our past. I became a storyteller and my children the eager listeners… Since my retirement in 1988 the Montreal Holocaust Museum became my home away from home. I still remember a very stormy day in February 1992, when a busload of Seventh Day Adventists, a church group, drove in from Cornwall, Ontario. After I finished telling my story there was complete silence, no visible reaction. A week later a parcel came to the Centre addressed to Renia. Inside the parcel there was a beautiful big doll and a letter telling me how sorry they are about my stolen childhood."*

Even after she died, I was able to check the facts with my mother.

Imelda Dickinson claimed to be a descendant of the nineteenth-century American poet Emily Dickinson. She claimed that she wrote poetry. Purportedly, her work-in-progress was a collection of poems telling the story of her dolls. Each poem was meant to tell the story of an individual doll. Imelda had sought out my mother in order to learn the story of the doll Mum named Ania.

"Do you know what happened to the doll?"

"Yes, of course. My mother kept it on her credenza for years. When she got sick, she took the doll with her on a trip to Poland and gave it to a friend for safekeeping, saying, "It's time for 'Ania' to come home.""

"Was Ania your mother's sister?"

"Yes."

"Do you know her story?"

"Of course I know my aunt's story."

In e-mails and phone calls I paid for, I sent Imelda full documents and extensive notes, speaking for two women who could no longer speak for themselves. When Imelda misheard Poland as Portugal and accepted it, I diplomatically gave her a Coles Notes version of modern European history.

In her search for my mother, Imelda stumbled upon a grieving daughter.

"I'm going to be your second mother. You call me at any time for anything. You're part of my family. You come here whenever you can and stay for as long as you want. You can stay with me forever! I love you, and I'm going to be your friend forever!"

Imelda began mailing commercial greeting cards, professing lifelong friendship and undying love. Into these cards she inserted lace doilies and glitter sticker butterflies. "You come to me and my family and we'll flood you with so much love that you won't be able to stand it. I have nine rooms. You have no excuse. After a visit with us, you will be restored!"

It was when Imelda began signing her e-mails "Love, Mom" that I gagged and asked her to desist. "My mother is irreplaceable. Please don't do it."

Miffed, the eighty-four-year-old Imelda modified her signature from Mom to Auntie.

The elderly Imelda bragged that she didn't take medication and never saw a doctor, so when she fell silent for an extended period in winter I worried and contacted her grandson Brad, who lived with her in the nine-room house.

Imelda was fine. "Oh dear, I've been so busy! I've been working on the book for twelve hours a day!" She was also preparing for her sister's wedding, and invited me. I received a flurry of e-mails telling me when to come and how to dress. "My family is your family. It would be so special if you would come and celebrate with us." That was before Imelda checked with her sister.

Imelda's eighty-year-old widowed sister was getting married to a former high school sweetheart who was now a widower. They were to be married on June 8.

"On the seventieth anniversary of D-Day." My mother's references had become mine.

"D-Day?" The Doll Lady queried. "What's that?"

Imelda asked me to send photographs of my mother in her youth so she could use them as the basis for the creation of a doll. She declared that she was going to design a doll to be called the Renia doll. "You'll pick up 'Renia' when you come here to visit. 'Renia' will fly home with you."

A pattern developed wherein periods of overwhelming attention was followed by extended and disturbing silences. When I was put on Neglect, I hung up. When I did, Imelda came after me, her Dotty-Old-Lady persona replaced by an astute human being. "I understand that you would be uncomfortable coming to someone you don't know. No one can ever replace Renia, Dear, and no one should. But there are people who would gladly enter your life and your heart, if you would only let them."

169

This was hard for me to believe. Upon Mum's death, what was covert became overt. Exclusion by the tribe was brutal and complete. Mark never knew the details of what transpired in Mum's apartment on the afternoon I threw Marty out of it. He didn't want to know. All that seemed to concern him was that I had been unpleasant to the man he considered his best friend.

Yet he had his best friend step down as back-up executor of Mum's estate. In effect, Mark overturned Mum's will in order to eliminate the danger of Marty gaining legal power over me. Mark finally recognized that Marty couldn't be trusted, though he refused to recognize how egregiously he had been betrayed. When Marty crossed the line, Mark moved the line. The two men and their families continued to socialize.

Laurie knew the details of that traumatic afternoon. He also knew its near-fatal consequences. Only Laurie kept contact with me.

All the while, the poetic descendant of Emily Dickinson painted tantalizing word pictures describing Wisconsin's fabled forests. Her daughter Julie, Brad's mother, lived in a fully equipped cabin in the woods, on forty acres of land populated with deer. Imelda owned the cabin and the land. "We'll bring you to the cabin. You'll sleep in the loft. You'll be surrounded by beauty, and you will have peace."

At first, Imelda suggested I come in summer. Plans changed when Brad's British girlfriend and her father announced they were coming for an extended stay. Imelda now suggested I come in September, and then she suggested I come in October. Again, I began pulling away.

"I'm afraid you're too busy for me."

"Dear, I intend to be busy until the day I die, and when you come I will be busy with you!"

Near the end of September Imelda finally settled on October 15 as an arrival date, but she would not give a definite return date. When I called her on a Sunday morning she erupted, "I can't talk to you now! I'm having breakfast in a restaurant and the waitress is bringing my food!"

In my head, an alarm went off. If only I had heeded it.

In early October, Imelda was still elusive. I got fed up. All night I agonized over the decision, and in the morning decided to cancel plans for the trip. In the afternoon I received an e-mail from Superior. "Book your return flight for November 2. Your bed is made and waiting for you."

November 2. The date slapped me in the face. The year before, the unveiling of the stone marking my mother's grave was held on November 2. This event, which Our Crowd calls An Unveiling, was actually a double unveiling. At Mum's request, Daddy's remains were exhumed and shipped to Ontario to lie beside her. You can't keep a good man down.

Mark didn't go so far as to bar me from the event, but he set conditions that he knew I would reject. "I can put you in a hotel near the cemetery and you can take the train back to Montreal immediately after the ceremony, or the next day. You are not welcome in our home." I studied Imelda's e-mail, and then called her.

"I am not a rich woman. Open tickets no longer exist. If you change your mind about the dates I will get stuck with a stiff financial penalty. You must be absolutely sure."

After hearing what I wanted to hear and lulled into believing that I was welcome in Imelda's nine-room home, with a heavy heart I booked the flights.

Outside Duluth's miniature airport, forty-five-year-old Brad was waiting by his car. Brad and his grandmother each had their own car. Brad was friendly, articulate, obese, and had a permanently swollen eye. He had recently relocated

171

from Hawaii back to Wisconsin. According to Brad, he came home to help his grandmother. According to The Doll Lady, Brad came home because of his health problem. The focus of Brad's health problem was his hyperactive eye, which mysteriously swelled at night, and receded during the day. Brad had gone as far as the Mayo Clinic in order to find out what was wrong with his eye, but to no avail. The disorder might've been easier to diagnose if a doctor had made a house call and examined Brad's mattress.

At The Doll Lady's request, on the way home we stopped at a restaurant located in a hotel. The Doll Lady ordered a pot of hot water with lemon and honey. Then she ordered a potato pancake, though those who celebrate Hanukkah would not have recognized it as such. A potato pancake in America's Upper Midwest is flat, thin, large, and as greasy as Vaseline. Brad ordered eggs that I believe are called Sunny Side Up, accompanied by hash brown potatoes, and a side order of two pancakes.

"Have a pancake, Grandma." Brad suddenly appeared to be watching his diet. "I only wanted one."

After the lunch I didn't participate in, we rode to The Doll Lady's home. It was a decrepit hundred-year-old house purchased less than two years before because, The Doll Lady explained, she didn't feel like living in her cabin anymore, and she resented the idea of paying rent. Instead, a woman in her eighties, still capable of driving, owner of a country home and forty acres of land sunk 50,000 dollars, which appeared to be her life savings, into a hundred-year-old house. The Doll Lady's plan; precisely, her fantasy, was to restore the house, sell it at a profit, and move to Hawaii with Brad and Brad's mother Julie. Why she simply hadn't sold the property, added the proceeds to her life savings and moved to Hawaii with her daughter, where her grandson was already established, was beyond me.

The house I entered may have been considered comfortable and elegant in 1915, but under The Doll Lady's stewardship the entire ground floor had been converted into storage space for three shops-full of what she called antiques, though much of the merchandise would've found appropriate homes in flea markets. The Doll Lady's daughter Julie owned and managed three antique shops, but had recently been turned out of them when the landlord she was renting from went bankrupt. "He over-invested," The Doll Lady scoffed. Over the course of the next few days, The Doll Lady would scoff a lot. There had been a dining room in the front part of the ground floor, and a fully equipped kitchen in the back. "I had the downstairs kitchen taken out," The Doll Lady airily explained. "I didn't like it." It wasn't clear who was paying for the renovations. One moment The Doll Lady cursed, "I've sunk five thousand into this house already, and now the workers are asking another five thousand, which I don't have!" The next moment, The Doll Lady was fine. "The State will pay for the renovations, because of my age."

The nine rooms contained in this crumbling mansion were a matter of opinion. At a stretch, counting both bathrooms and the upstairs kitchen, which had a slanted floor and no table nor chairs, one might count nine rooms, though few were usable, and not all of them had doors.

The room I was assigned to sleep in had no door. One might describe it as an alcove, though it didn't lead anywhere, except to an outdoor ledge. The Doll Lady used it as her sewing room. It held a small and lumpy sofa, a large and lumpy armchair, a large, wide screen TV used to screen videos (there was no TV service) and a small hard-backed, unarmed chair. There were two small drawers under the TV, and one was stuffed with face cloths. I was told that these drawers were assigned to me for the duration of my stay. Brad suggested to his grandmother that I might need a regular-sized towel to wrap myself in, after taking a shower. That's when I was handed a towel.

There was no closet, so there was no need for hangers until I got there. I asked where I could hang my clothes. Imelda supplied a metal rod with holes that she inserted into the door that led to the ledge she described as a "deck".

The alcove was carpeted, and the carpet was visibly unvacuumed. In the centre of the debris-encrusted carpet sat a metal child-sized cot stuffed with filthy foam and a stained and ripped mattress. A pretty quilt, like make-up on a dirty face, covered the mattress and the foam. A dusty pillow topped this contraption. The Doll Lady had made my bed, and I was expected to lie in it.

I had just spent the day traveling. The only food I had was the food I packed for myself since I divined, from e-mails sent after I finally booked the flight, that there would be no food prepared for me. After dissolving powdered broth into a cup of hot water and drinking it, I removed the pillow, the quilt, the mattress and the foam, folded up the cot, and placed the bedding on the floor. "Oh I feel terrible." The Doll Lady paid lip service to the discomfort she had created.

"I guess you didn't realize how tall I am." I was diplomatic. I was also stuck. I was allowed to move the cot onto the "deck".

"We were going to throw it out after you left, anyway," The Doll Lady declared, without embarrassment. Still, I was not allowed to place the hard-backed chair outside. "It might rain." The Doll Lady warned. It was a moot point. Once the cot was placed onto the deck, there was room for no one and nothing else. The Doll Lady folded the narrow mattress and tossed it onto the sofa, next to my suitcase. "I can sell it at our next garage sale," she said, and believed what she said.

"Oh I don't think anyone will buy that." The words fell out of my mouth before I could stop them.

"You wouldn't believe what people will buy!" The Doll Lady harrumphed. She was right. I not only wouldn't believe what people might buy, I also had a hard time believing how outrageously the public's intelligence can be insulted by what people might dare try to sell.

As I lay with clenched shoulders on the too-narrow mattress, The Doll Lady brought in her dinner on a tray and perched on the edge of the hard-backed chair which held my carry-on case, eating and chatting, while I lay exhausted at her feet. My closed eyes began to itch and tear. I knew what was happening but was helpless to do anything about it, that evening. By morning not only were my shoulders, neck and jaw in spasm, but my eyes were almost as swollen as Brad's, my head felt swollen, my lungs felt congested, and my throat was not only sore, but also raw. Mould and dust mites were causing this reaction.

I asked to be taken to Walmart, which I had seen on the way in, in order to purchase a new pillow and a sleeping bag.

"I hate Walmart." The Doll Lady scorned the mega store. "If you have all these allergies then you should do a three-day detox!" The Doll Lady diagnosed, prescribed, and dismissed.

We discussed possible options, as well as impossible options.

"Julie had a sleeping bag, but I don't think she has it anymore. She has an air mattress, but it keeps losing air."

We went downstairs and perused the three shops-full of merchandise to see if anything was usable. I spied a large mattress at the far end of what may have once been a back parlour. "I can sleep on that," I declared, with relief. "It's large enough." The mattress certainly was large. It was far

175

too large for an old and a middle-aged woman to haul up a flight of stairs, and according to The Doll Lady, Brad couldn't be disturbed. He had already put himself out carrying my suitcase up the stairs, and I wasn't to ask for anything more.

"If the mattress can't come to me, then I can come to the mattress!" Once more, I felt inspired. Reluctantly The Doll Lady allowed me to move downstairs, but she wouldn't allow her space heater to accompany me.

"It costs 350 dollars. I can't risk its being broken."

The back area containing the mattress also housed a second bathroom. Its bathtub was stuffed with pieces of small furniture, and its shower hose didn't work because, The Doll Lady sneered, Brad's girlfriend's eighty-year-old father had broken it during their stay in the summer. Reggie was disabled. Reggie was in a wheelchair. During their stay, it was Reggie who used the large mattress. He also used the downstairs bathroom, and had latched onto the shower hose in order to haul himself off the toilet. That's how he broke it.

"That idiot. Using a shower hose to get off a toilet. It would cost fifty dollars to replace. I'm not going to spend fifty dollars to replace a shower hose. Dumb. Dumb. Brad won't marry Gemma unless she leaves her father. Gemma won't leave Reggie because he's disabled, but I don't think he's as badly off as she makes out. He's just selfish. And dumb."

If The Doll Lady had no sympathy for an eighty-year-old man in a wheelchair, she wasn't about to develop any for me. I had not only flown to Wisconsin in good faith, I had arrived in good shape. In conditions created by The Doll Lady, this wouldn't last long.

The back corner of the back parlour not only held a mattress, but there was a desk beside it, and a working lamp. The mattress was wedged between the desk and an empty bookcase. There was a stack of books behind the desk. There was a sink and toilet in the downstairs bathroom, both of which worked. It was decided that I would sleep here and do my living upstairs. To compensate for the space heater I was denied, Imelda wheeled out something that looked like a truncated radiator, with a plug. It worked, but the only thing this item heated was itself. It was so cold in that corner, so very cold. Imelda supplied extra blankets but they froze, along with the pillow she finally allowed me to purchase at Walmart. In an effort to get warm, I would resort to placing the pillow and the bottom sheet on the portable radiator-contraption. I may have been risking a fire but by then, I barely cared.

After my sleeping arrangements were altered to the best that The Doll Lady would allow, we drove to the local supermarket for groceries. Imelda instructed me to get a cart for myself and meet her after I finished shopping and most particularly, after I finished paying. Imelda shopped for herself.

I had written in an e-mail that I could make a meal out of a baked potato and yogurt. In this, The Doll Lady took me at my word. She bought a sack of potatoes because she used them too, but I supplied my own yogurt. Since The Doll Lady let me know that we have certain food preferences in common, I bought these items in order to share them with her. I would ultimately enrich The Doll Lady's kitchen.

Brad's food was stored on the top shelf of the refrigerator because "he can't bend", and I shared the lower shelf with The Doll Lady. I received a dirty look when I added three carrots to my nightly meal of a potato and yogurt. I survived The Doll Lady's dirty look, as I survived the dirt in the rest of the house. I was hungry.

177

On the second night I wrapped myself in blankets, on the mattress in what I imagined was once a back parlour. I had light to read by. I had books to read. I had a bathroom to myself. There was more shelf space in the desk where I could store my belongings than there had been in the drawers under the TV upstairs. There was no door, but I was far enough removed so that I had privacy. I surveyed the piles of furniture in the dark and decrepit house and tried to imagine that I was sleeping in Dickens' *Old Curiosity Shop.*

If only I could get warm, I could make this visit work. I wondered if Imelda would let me buy an electric heating pad. Then I remembered that it isn't safe to sleep with a switched-on electric heating pad. I wondered if Imelda would let me buy a hot water bottle. I could place it at my feet, but its warmth wouldn't last the night. Could she be induced into making another trip to Walmart, where I could buy a space heater? I would leave it behind, as I would leave the pillow behind. There would be more for her to sell.

As the damp and rattling cold entered my muscles and bones, I thought of my mother huddling under a coat on a mattress in an apartment in winter, in the Warsaw Ghetto. She and her sister shared one pair of shoes, and they took turns venturing into the streets in order to forage for food. As my shoulders and neck and skull went into spasm I thought of the hypothermia that killed concentration camp inmates on death marches. It was the second night of my long-awaited vacation, and that is how my mind was working.

In the middle of the night, no longer able to lie on my frozen back, I rolled over onto my side and my knee struck one of the shelves of the empty bookcase. The blow woke me, and my knee swelled. That is when I began to cry.

Imelda found me in the morning, bent over my swollen knee. "I don't believe it!" She ridiculed. Another dumb and clumsy guest. There was no ice in the freezer, though behind Imelda's back I retrieved a sack of frozen vegetables and applied it to my swollen knee. In the immediate aftermath of the injury the health educator applied an herbal ointment to it, wrapped my kneecap in gauze, and then covered all with an ace bandage. I asked if I might have the use of a cane. I suspected there might be one on the premises. "Sure. The State gave me a cane, because of my age. I have no intention of using it. You can use the cane."

As I sat upstairs in the lumpy armchair with my leg lifted onto a box, Imelda handed me a list of activities and tourist attractions that were supposedly free. Brad's girlfriend in England had prepared the list. I wasn't interested in attending high school choir performances. What I did find of interest was deemed either too far, not interesting, or had a nominal charge, which I was prepared to pay, but Imelda was not. (The Doll Lady ignored my offer to pay entrance fees for her.)

In the afternoon Imelda drove us to Duluth, to its port on Lake Superior. The autumn leaves were at their peak. The air was bracing, the seagulls whirled in a sky clear and deeply blue, the great lake was an even deeper blue and smelled like the seaports in Greece. There was no entrance fee, but there was a parking fee. Stepping on the gas whose price she complained about, Imelda managed to avoid paying the fee.

On Sunday, Imelda drove me to a state park that boasted the highest waterfalls in Wisconsin. She sat in the car, reading and sewing because she found it difficult to walk, so she said.

According to the printout provided, entrance to the state park was free. According to the attendant who stopped us at the gate, it was not. "Have you got three dollars?" Imelda turned to me. I did, and I had no problem handing it over.

On the way back from the park, we stopped at the local supermarket. I hadn't prepared enough money to buy groceries. I didn't know we were going to make the stop.

"Do you stop at the supermarket often," I asked, wanting to be prepared.

"I get in my groceries once a month!" Imelda huffed. "The reason I'm going so often now is because of you!"

Over the phone, Imelda had told me that she served as caregiver to a sister-in-law, the sister of her first husband. "I've buried three husbands, and the next one will bury me!" I knew the stories of Husband Number One and Husband Number Three. I also knew the story of the married man who fathered her first daughter when she was seventeen. Thirty years later, The Doll Lady's discovery of the child she had been forced to relinquish led to the meeting with Husband Number Three. I did not know the story of Husband Number Two, so I asked.

"I left him after two weeks because he wouldn't sleep with me. He was sleeping with his son. My second husband was a widower. He told me his son hadn't gotten over the loss of his mother and couldn't be left alone at night, so he was sleeping with him, and not with me. So I said to him, 'Why did we get married?' "

Why, indeed. So I wasn't the first. It appeared Imelda had no qualms about seducing the bereaved.

"Is your second husband still alive?"

"I don't know and I couldn't care less." Neither was there any sympathy for the boy who had lost his mother.

There were many discrepancies in the tales Imelda told me over the phone calls I was sponsoring, and the versions I heard in person. My head spun as I tried to match what was unmatchable. Imelda did serve as a caregiver to her sister-in-law. An agency funded by the state of Wisconsin was paying her ten dollars an hour to shop, clean house, and serve a woman who had Alzheimer's disease. Imelda ran the errands, put in her time, and clocked in with the agency. This meant she was out for several hours each day. When I first arrived, we stopped at a hardware store because Imelda had lost the key to her house. When the new key was cut, she handed it to me. How was she able to cut a copy of a lost key? I was confused. I was in a constant state of confusion. I thought Imelda was handing me a copy to keep for the duration of my stay. No, there was to be only one key, and we would share it. Though Brad stayed home, working at his computer all day, and then skyped his British girlfriend into the evening and half the night, I was forbidden to knock on the front door when Imelda was out so that I wouldn't disturb him. I offered to pay to have another key made.

"I don't want to drive back to the hardware store to make a copy of the key," Imelda stated firmly. And anyway," Imelda continued, not so firmly, "Julie doesn't allow it. With all her merchandise in the house, no one is allowed to have a copy of the keys except family."

As if I would stuff the contents of three antique shops into my suitcase, on top of my clothes. Imelda used Julie as an excuse whenever she felt in need of one.

On Monday morning Imelda offered, without enthusiasm, "I can take you to where the boat cruises are, but I won't go with you."

When I first arrived Imelda told me there were sightseeing excursions on the lake, but the season had ended and the boats were no longer sailing. I couldn't understand why she would tell me about it if I couldn't make use of the information but then, I noticed a pattern developing in which Imelda would hand me a menu, and then snatch away the meal. Now she was telling me that the boats were sailing. I suspected it was because she recognized that I was prepared to pay my way.

"But Imelda, it's raining." I would've loved to go cruising on a *bateau mouche* but my cold and cramped muscles didn't relish the prospect of being battered by the wind and rain, nor even sitting trapped in a glass shelter.

"Is it? Well, that's that, then."

"When's Julie coming?" I offered, for something to say.

"Well she can't come now because you're here! I hadn't planned on your being downstairs! Julie needs to sell her merchandise, and she can't get any work done if you're here."

I only slept downstairs; I wasn't living there.

"Imelda, I came on your time, on your schedule, on the dates that you gave me. Now you're telling me I'm in the way. I'm scheduled to be here for another two weeks. If I'm in your daughter's way then where should I go and what should I do?"

"Well the merchandise has to be sold. I can't help that. You can go back upstairs! I have neighbours who are always asking what they can do for me! I'll call them and ask them to bring the mattress upstairs."

This was a switch. When I mentioned to Imelda that I had fallen into conversation with a neighbour on my daily walks she erupted, "Oh I don't talk to my neighbours. I don't want to have anything to do with them. They loved the previous owner of this house, and he lied to me about its condition. They wish he was still here, and not me!" Suddenly she had neighbours so accommodating that she was sure they would drag a mattress up a flight of stairs. She was right. A young couple came in the evening and cheerfully brought the mattress up to the alcove. Then the man turned to Imelda, grinned, and informed her, almost proudly, "I had a stroke last month!" When they left, Imelda

182

turned on me. "That man had a heart attack. If I had known I never would've asked him to bring up the mattress for you"

After sending me back upstairs Imelda then let me know, "I have to go to the cabin on Wednesday and haul wood for Julie. I'll be coming back on Thursday." An eighty-five-year-old woman hauled wood for her sixty-two-year-old daughter because her daughter was disabled. Julie had a metal plate in her neck, though I never understood why. In pictures I'd seen of her, she was seated in a wheelchair. It looked like the same wheelchair that had crashed onto the back of my legs after my knee was injured. Between the plate in Julie's neck and Brad's rebellious eye, it appeared the only able-bodied person on the dangerously overstuffed premises was the eighty-five-year-old Imelda.

Once more, my head spun. If the mattress was being moved upstairs to accommodate Julie, then who was coming or going to whom? I understood that we, both of us, were to be heading out to Smokey the Bear country, to the fully equipped cabin with the forty acres of land where deer, and perhaps antelope, play. I was to sleep in a loft. I was to be surrounded by beauty and peace. According to the most recent e-mails, there was a bed waiting for me there, too.

"You're going alone? I understood that I was invited too."

"Well, in the kind of shape you're in, you can't even haul a log of wood."

"Imelda, I'm a human being. I've been injured. I need a chance to recover."

"You can recover at home."

Now I was more than confused. Now I was shocked. I knew Imelda's irresponsibility wasn't personal. She dealt in distortion. Her choices were mindless. She thought nothing through, whether it was buying a house or housing a guest. Still, I couldn't fully grasp the horror of having been sucked into the orbit of an elderly *enfant terrible* who picked up people like dolls, played with them, petted them, damaged them, and then discarded them. The creature was grotesque, and I had placed myself at her mercy.

I said nothing. My hostess refused to keep me warm and safe, and seemed to resent my attempts at taking care of myself. Insult had been added to injury. I limped away. I didn't call the emergency number on the enhanced travel and medical insurance policy I bought before making the trip. I didn't believe my injury was serious enough to require treatment nor "travel interruption", and I didn't know enough to ask.

In the afternoon the sky cleared and, sporting Imelda's cane, I went for a walk. The morning had been unpromising. Mid-afternoon morphed into a lovely, mild, Indian summer of a day. Residents in the neighbourhood were out on the streets. A gentleman sitting on his porch hailed me.

"Beautiful day, isn't it?"

"Indeed." Our eyes locked. What caught Frank's attention was the cane.

"Are you alright?"

"Oh, that's a loaded question." I approached Frank's porch. He was a disabled Army veteran living in a fourplex. His rent was subsidized by what the state called assisted housing. He had destroyed both his knees jumping out of planes. I believe other parts of his anatomy had been damaged by similar feats of derring-do.

Spending the afternoon with Frank was a relief. I was parched for intelligent conversation. Frank told me his story, and I told him mine.

"I'm trying to make a decision whether to stay or leave."

His nods and grimaces confirmed what I knew. The aptly named Frank didn't tell me what I wanted to hear; he told me what I needed to hear. "As long as you're here, you're homeless. This woman hasn't been dealing in good faith. You've been deceived."

When I returned to The Doll Lady's house I had to bang heavily on the door in order to be let in. The Doll Lady was home, but she had locked me out. I recognized the gesture as punishment for having dared to ask for a copy of the house keys.

When Imelda let me in she also let me know that her daughter Julie "really wanted you to come and visit the cabin. You weren't invited just so you could haul wood."

"I know." Of course I knew. I believed Julie's invitation was sincere. It was Imelda who had reneged. I could also imagine what she must have told her daughter about me. The invitation was not reinstated.

Imelda then offered to show me pictures of the cabin and the land and the deer. Once more the menu was replacing the meal. I declined Imelda's offer as respectfully as I could.

While I had the time on the mattress downstairs, and when Imelda was out, I made several calls to Laurie in Toronto. I had purchased a cell phone plan as well as a calling card, to be used as a back-up, in case I felt the need to make a very long long-distance call to Canada. I never used the calling card. I stuck to the use of my cell phone, because I was afraid to touch Imelda's phone. She might walk in, and catch me at it. I had become afraid.

Before I left, Laurie wrote to me, "I hope you have an amazing trip, but don't take crap from anybody. If anyone gives you a hard time you just call us and me or Mark will fly down there and bring you home!" There was unintended irony in Laurie's offer. At the time it was made, I didn't take it seriously. After three days in The Doll Lady's domain, I was taking Laurie's offer very seriously, indeed.

When I called him on it, Laurie's flamboyant promise transmuted into a subdued, "Sometimes you've just got to bite the bullet." Laurie was prepared to assist in finding a flight home, but I would have to pay for it.

"Don't tell my brother." I was embarrassed that I had fallen into such a trap. I didn't want Mark to know that I had volunteered for victimization. It is unnecessary to blame the victim. Victims are quick to blame themselves.

"I've already contacted Mark." Laurie informed me. To my amazement, he added, "No one's judging."

Mark and Laurie manned their computers and began searching for flights out. The financial penalty was egregious. I was loath to pay it.

I tried to make the best of an unjust situation. The Doll Lady remained intransigent. Why shouldn't she? The risk had been mine, the expense had been mine, the effort had been mine, and now the hardship was mine.

On Monday night, back upstairs in the alcove, on the large mattress, I gave up trying to sleep as Brad's voice cut through his door and wafted into the space where I lay. He was on Skype with his girlfriend in London. Brad worked at his computer during the day, skyped his British girlfriend from four to nine in the evening, went out for a walk after nine and then returned to his computer, where he continued skyping until two in the morning. He rose at noon, which is when his day began. Unless he had to leave the premises for an appointment, Brad adhered to this routine seven days a week, except for December, when he flew to London.

After a sleepless night, in the morning, I lay on the mattress overhearing Imelda on the telephone. There was a call made to a store, informing them to cancel the order she had placed for bulbs to be planted in her garden. "Don't send me any more flowers!" There was a call made to a doctor's office, shifting blame onto the bank for a twenty-three-dollar cheque that bounced. Then the poor old woman decided to have new windows installed in a house even older than she was.

There were no more offers, even half-hearted ones, to take me, or send me, sightseeing. I had been forced back to the second floor of the house, even though having to climb up and down the stairs was preventing the healing of my knee. I was picking up texts from Mark giving me options for flights back to Canada. "Mum's estate will pay." So Mark said, but I suspected differently. Imelda was pointedly letting me know that I was unwelcome. I posed the question, prepared for the answer.

"Do you want me to leave?"

"Yes!" The Doll Lady erupted, with hostility, and relief. "You're having an unpleasant time here. You're not feeling well. You should go home and recover. You should recover at home." It was a masterful evasion of responsibility. It was also brutal.

"Thanks, MOM!"

The Doll Lady's eyes popped. I stomped off, retrieved my cell phone, a pen and a notebook, hobbled downstairs to The Old Curiosity Shop, and called my brother. Imelda followed me. I set my cell phone on Speaker mode. Deliberately.

"There's a flight out tomorrow." Mark's stern tone struck the eavesdropping Doll Lady. "It's a morning flight. You'd have a fifty-minute stopover in Chicago. Your connecting flight would be in another terminal. Want me to book it?"

"Fifty minutes to get to another terminal in Chicago? That airport is massive! I'll never make it! Should I move to a hotel for a couple of days?" Hovering among the junk in The Old Curiosity Shop, The Doll Lady bristled.

"Look," Mark countered. He is a far more experienced and frequent flyer than I. His authoritative physician's voice brought The Doll Lady to attention. "If it weren't feasible the airlines wouldn't schedule it that way. If you don't make the connecting flight, it's the airline's responsibility to get you onto the next flight. Under the circumstances, it's the best I can do. I'm booking it, and I can't buy a third ticket!" As I suspected, it was Mark who was funding my escape. "You will not have to spend more than this night in that house!" Mark blasted. The Doll Lady bridled at my brother's bark of disgust. "You're getting out of there!"

In that moment, both The Doll Lady and I learned that I wasn't alone in the world. In a modern twist on a grim fairy-tale, it was Hansel who was rescuing Gretel from the house of a witch.

I hobbled upstairs to retrieve my suitcase, dragged it down to The Old Curiosity Shop, and then made several trips up and down the stairs to retrieve my belongings. It was easier to bring down an empty suitcase rather than a full one and Brad, of course, could not be disturbed.

I packed. The Doll Lady eyed me like a wary fox. When I returned upstairs, Brad had emerged from his lair and was in the kitchen. I asked him for the number of a taxi.

"Noela, if you want to go somewhere I can drive you."

Brad was pleasant enough when he was allowed near me. It was the cunning Doll Lady who kept her pawns separate and apart.

"I need to get to the airport tomorrow morning."

Brad backed off. Disturbed, he stared at his silent grandmother. Then he retreated to his room. Brad was not prepared to drive me to the airport. His loyalty lay with his grandmother. At his computer, he retrieved the number of a cab company. That was the most he could bring himself to do.

When I finished packing, I picked up the cane Imelda didn't use and went for a walk in order to get away from this house of horrors, in which dead objects are sheltered and protected, and a living human being is damaged, devalued, and tossed. The Doll Lady's perverted values seemed merely an extreme of what I was seeing around me, in this ironically named town. Everyone had at least one car, because it was impossible to function without one. Almost everyone had a house, but not all householders had the resources to comfortably maintain their dwellings so they bundled up, living in the dark and sleeping in the cold, in order not to run up heat and electricity bills. From what I could see, the residents of Superior were enslaved by their stuff. It was the underbelly of The American Dream.

The wind whipped up. Dead leaves whirled. Behind neighbouring fences dogs snarled and leapt to the railings, menacing me.

I didn't take a taxi to the airport. Imelda assured me that she would drive me there. As little as she could be trusted, I trusted her to get me to the airport because I knew how badly she wanted me to leave. When I returned from my walk, Imelda offered to make a salad for me. I declined. She offered to take me with her on an errand she was running for her sister-in-law. She even offered to drive me to Walmart. I was on the verge of declining when I decided to accept. There was no point in resisting The Doll Lady.

It had been a blustery day. After running the errand for her sister-in-law, Imelda drove me to the bay. She wanted to share the sunset. In the tangled branches of Imelda's mind, cloudy days were the best days to view sunsets. Over a lawn littered with Canadian geese, the last of the day's sun oozed through wads of clouds, like an open wound. As we sat in the car, Imelda indicated the sites of this town with the arrogant name.

"That's the widow's peak in the mansion I pointed out to you on the first day. You would've gotten to visit it, if you weren't leaving."

On Tuesday morning, Imelda dropped me off at the airport in Duluth. "Would you like me to come in and wait with you?"

I was beyond amazement. On the way in, a large sign clearly stated hourly parking rates. Was she really willing to pay two dollars for parking?

"It isn't necessary." Then I thanked The Doll Lady for the only thing it was possible to thank her for. "Thank you for sending my brother back to me."

Imelda looked forlorn. Quickly, I turned away. I couldn't afford to feel sorry for The Doll Lady. She had cost me too much.

I never saw Imelda's book. When I asked, she told me, "Oh I made some copies and gave them to people who have dolls." When I asked to see the poem she wrote based on the story of the doll she gave my mother, she shrugged, "It's somewhere in the computer. I'll have to dig it out." She never did. As for the Renia doll; it never materialized.

I flew from Duluth to Chicago. In The Windy City's massive airport, I approached an official. "Is there a GO cart that can drive me to Terminal Two?"

"There is, but it won't leave for another twenty minutes, and if you've got a connecting flight in fifty minutes you'll get there more quickly if you walk."

Wheeling my carry-on case and disregarding the pain in my knee, I did not walk. I dashed. Past gaudy souvenir stands and fast food joints I ran a relay race among international travellers and flight personnel. With my head held high in order to read directions and signs, I flew through Terminal One like one of the jets landing outside the windows. Angels seemed to fly beside me as I wound my way through the maze of Chicago's O'Hare Airport. With ten minutes to spare, the Air Canada gate came into sight. Breathing heavily, I flung myself into the line forming in front of the gate.

"Relax Lady! You made it!" A U.S. airport official smiled.

On the wall alongside the ramp leading to the interior of the plane there was a sign that read, NOW. Move Forward. With Confidence.

In early evening, I reached my suburban Montreal apartment. I let go of baggage and went out into the busy and darkened streets. It was October 21. Election posters of the borough's mayor gleamed under lighted lamp posts. He had just been elected to Parliament. Within less than a week I left a country living under a conservative government and returned to a country with a Prime Minister Trudeau. Again.

There was a police cordon around City Hall. Blue-collar workers were holding a meeting, and it was expected that they might stage a protest.

In the local library, there were lectures and concerts. In the neighbourhood cinema, ballets were beamed in by satellite from Moscow, operas were offered from New York, and plays were projected from London. There was movement. There was life. For the first time in a long time, I felt part of it. Before going to bed I sent an e-mail to my brother. *Thank you for bringing me home.*

FINDING MY FEET

The Laurentian Hills, Quebec – The autumn and winter of 2016-2017

The Doll Lady taught me the dangers of isolation. Still reeling from the trauma of the recent past, I joined a hiking club. The most I hoped for was to sit quietly on a yellow school bus as it transported into the countryside a group of active senior citizens. I still paid full price for everything, so I don't know how I came to be considered a senior citizen, but in certain milieu, I was. Perhaps I was a junior senior.

On the first Friday morning I arrived at the Come-On-In Centre for Seniors, a member of the club noticed me hanging back in a corner of the cafeteria, clutching my new knapsack. I was more nervous that morning than on my first day of kindergarten. "Come on in!" she called. "The water's fine!"

At half past eight on Friday mornings, we were ready to roll. At two o'clock on Friday afternoons, we'd haul our exhausted carcasses back onto the bus. Ouf!

On the bus, I discovered that I could comfortably socialize. On the trails, I was startled to discover how frightened I had become of downward slopes. As I stiffened and inched along a hand reached from behind, gently nudging the back side of my forearm and guiding my direction. "Why are you afraid?" The warm, dark-honeyed voice of one of the fitness trainers who leads these outings, asked rhetorically. Why, indeed? I came to think of these trainers as good shepherds who would not allow a lamb to slip over the side of a hill.

Beguiled by the beauty of the views I moved forward, often tentative, on occasion with budding assurance, sometimes tripping over the exposed root of an ancient maple, always grateful to be breathing cedar-scented air. Lunchtime would find me stretched out on a rock or a dock or a picnic bench by a rushing gorge or a sun-dappled lake.

When autumn turned to winter we strapped snowshoes onto our boots, and the lunches we carried in our knapsacks were consumed in huts, by the amber-coloured flames of log-burning wood stoves. The first time my feet entered one of these contraptions I felt like I would topple over. Along with my stance, I had to adjust my attitude. "Stomp, Noela, stomp your feet!" the head shepherd instructed. "The reason you feel like you're falling is because you aren't stepping forcefully. The snowshoes have clamps. They'll bite the ground and hold you up. Stomp! Noela! Stomp!" So I stomped and I clomped, feeling like The Abominable Snowman. Climbing uphill was hard, but not frightening. The effort felt familiar. In a sense, I'd been climbing uphill all my life.

Sometimes we tramped in wide meadows surrounded by taupe-coloured trees, and sometimes we edged our way through narrow paths in a snow-laden glade I dubbed The Land of Sugar-Frosted Pines. Once, we entered a region in the Laurentians called Farhills. These hills were not only far; they were steep. My fellow hikers had to be helped down the icy and treacherous trail, so what chance did I have? When my turn came, I gauged the conditions and made my choice. "Screw this." A fine line separates courage from stupidity, and I was on the verge of crossing it. I plunked down onto the ground before falling down, raised my snowshoe-clad feet in the air, tossed my hiking sticks away from me, shoved at the snow with my gloves and whizzed down the slope, the ice under my behind serving as a natural toboggan. Two alarmed female shepherds dashed down the hill – they were the only ones capable of doing so. "Noela! Are you alright?!"

I thrust out my arms and exulted, through crystallized breath, "It's the only way to travel!"

Having flown down the hill, literally, by the seat of my pants, I faced another challenge. How to stand up? My feet flailed in the air. They were trapped in the snowshoes. "I need to get these things off."

"No you don't," the shepherds corrected. "We'll get you on your feet."

"You can't." I bleated. "I'm too heavy."

"Oh yes we can!" Shepherd Annette positioned herself on one side of me; Shepherd Jayne positioned herself on the other. "As we lift, you push. Push from your knees, Noela! Push!" So saying, they heaved, I ho-ed, and up I sprang! I grinned at the good shepherds in admiration and awe. Not only was I on my feet; I was also smiling.

By late afternoon we were back in the city. I returned to my apartment, soaked in a warm, sea-salted bath, and in sweet exhaustion fell into bed. My body burned, my muscles ached, and I slept like one of the logs that occasionally crossed our paths on the hiking trails.

MOUNTAIN GUIDE

L'Esterel, Quebec and Montreal, Quebec – The late winter of 2017 and Christmas Time, 1965

"Don't worry Noela. He's behind you." Jayne meant to reassure me. Instead, I got nervous. Then she raced up a trail to lead the rest of the group. It seemed I was being given special consideration because I was the slowest of the slow.

"This is a beautiful way to start the day, isn't it?" The warm, dark-honeyed voice from behind attempted to make conversation.

It was the twelfth anniversary of Mum's cancer diagnosis. It would soon be the thirty-fifth anniversary of Daddy's untimely death. It was also a glorious middle March morning in the Laurentian Hills and a younger man, not yet fifty, was guiding me through the woods. Some forms of pain are so deep that they are best addressed through physical exertion.

"Yes, it's a good morning."

That was a non-starter.

"Have you seen any animals on the trails?" The warm, dark-honeyed voice from behind took another tack.

"None so far."

"So far? There don't seem to be any. They seem to be hiding."

The woods were still, and the cedars and evergreens cast shadows. In our snowshoes we clomped along the twisting trails through the shadows, traversing what was transforming into an enchanted forest.

Dark Honey was familiar with the terrain. Anticipating an abrupt divide, he cautioned, "We're about to reach a fork in the road."

"Which way do we turn?" I asked my guide.

Dark Honey hesitated before deciding. "You choose. I'll follow you."

With my guide guarding my back, I turned towards True North.

"A jug of wine…" I whispered, to myself.

"A loaf of bread.'" Not only was Dark Honey's hearing acute, but he also knew the quote.

And thou beside me singing in the wilderness, I thought, but dared not say. The only way to preserve this sweet moment was to keep it to myself.

"What are you reading these days, Noela?"

"I'm reading a book called *Nice Girls Finish Fat.* Nothing you could relate to."

Early on Dark Honey pegged me that most startling of creatures; an intellectual. I can't imagine why. Could it be because he's a fitness trainer? It's not as if he's a jock. There are times when he comes across as a jock and one could be forgiven for thinking him a jock. Yet he's not. Nor am I an intellectual, dammit.

Dark Honey's attempt at conversation skidded to a halt. Granted, I hadn't made it easy. In companionable silence we hiked along our serpentine trail through benign shadows shot through with sunlight. At intervals, our silence and the silence of the woods were punctuated by the sound of Dark Honey humming to himself. When Dark Honey hums in the woods, one knows all is well.

As I wobbled down a slippery slope; Dark Honey flitted in front and talked me to level ground. When he was sure that I was safe, he darted ahead. I plodded along on my own, and then looked up to see him poised next to a log, one lean leg stretched and bent in front of the other, with his finely-shaped head turned and focused on me. His black-and-red striped tuque hugged his dark curls and a bolt of exposed red scarf flashed at his throat. Dark Honey looked like a large bird suspended in flight. Suspended in flight and animation because he was waiting for me. Be still, my heart.

As I tottered toward this vision, one of my snowshoes slipped off. Dark Honey dashed toward me, knelt at my feet, removed his thick gloves, and began to secure the racquet-shaped shoe to my hiking boot. Most women relish having a man at their feet, but I was uncomfortable. I bent and tried to assist. "No Noela. I'll take care of it." So I stood like a helpless child, gazing down on Dark Honey as his pale, tapering fingers tightened and worked metal attachments into tough rubber straps. A sleeve on his jacket lifted. Shafts of sunshine filtered through the sheltering trees, onto our meandering path. The silver metal band of his wristwatch glittered in glints of cold winter sun.

My gaze fixed on the face of the watch. These days, few men wear such watches. Its second hand ticked quickly, but its minute hand trolled slowly, as if resisting the passage of time. Through the boughs of snow-laden evergreens I detected Daddy's long-stilled tenor whispering, "*Shepsaleh*. The days are long, but the years are short..." In this enchanted forest, our sinuous trail slithered into the distant past. Into the dead of winter. On a Saturday morning...

On Saturday afternoon I was scheduled to perform in a children's theatre production at Victoria Hall. The drama queen in me is tempted to declare that a storm was raging but truth be told, the blizzard had passed. Our cosy corner of North America was transformed into a dark and deserted region of mountainous snow. The *metro* system did not yet exist. Neither did snowploughs. The buses weren't rolling. The buses weren't moving. Nothing was moving. Or so it seemed.

My parents and I were huddled around the kitchen table.

Breakfast was over, but argument was not. Mum insisted that I stay home.

"Daddy can't take the car. He'll get stuck. No one will show up anyway. You can't go."

I was mortified. "But I have to! If I don't show up, they'll never give me another part!" I stopped short of saying, "And I'll never work in the theatre again!" But I did proclaim, "The show must go on." Our teachers at *The Montreal's Children's Theatre* had taught us that. I was an impressionable little thespian. I was also a quick study.

With the edge of a long silver spoon, Daddy pressed a slice of lemon against the inside of his glass of tea. My sense of responsibility made him smile. It also prompted him to rise from the table, enter the hallway, and pull on his heavy boots, his warm jacket, and the silly hat with the big floppy ear flaps.

"*Mishigah*!" Mum wailed, instantly deciphering the intentions behind Daddy's actions. "Abram! What are you doing?" Mum wasn't asking. "You can't do it." Now Mum made her meaning clear. "You won't make it!"

"Well we can't let the child go by herself! And besides," Daddy raised his arm and waggled a forefinger, "The show, it has to go on!"

Daddy was a Polish Jew who survived the war years in Siberia. The prospect of trekking from the Cote des Neiges area to Westmount didn't faze him. He was also an older parent. When I was ten, my daddy was almost fifty. But he was a tough and strong Almost Fifty. Mum was overruled.

In late morning we set out into the empty streets, my small mitted hand resting in Daddy's large gloved hand. What confronted us was a wonderland. Ropes of snow rimmed bare branches, like sugar frosting. Caps of snow perched on spiked fences, like ice cream in cones. What looked like white sculptures turned out to be cars buried under snow. Despite the early hour street lamps switched on, as if ignited by an attentive elf.

A gust of wind whistled at the snow, startling it off rooftops. Particles of snow, transformed into silver sequins, pirouetted under the illuminated lamps. Smoke curled out of chimneys in crayoned pearl grey swirls. Formless clouds smudged the sky. Traffic lights were the only spots of colour in a magical, monochrome world.

Generally I was a chatterbox, but now I knew to conserve my energy and hold my peace. In companionable silence I trudged beside my dad. Sometimes I hiked behind him as he marched through deep drifts, creating a trail for me to follow. I raised my knees high and plunked down my feet in the imprints of my father's footsteps. My feet hurt because my feet were flat, like my daddy's feet. But Daddy didn't complain, so neither did I. When snow banks proved too high, Daddy lifted me over them. When wind currents proved too powerful, Daddy pulled me through them.

It was early afternoon when we reached the invisible border that divides Notre Dame de Grace from Westmount. Curtains of clouds parted, and sunshine tossed a spotlight onto a fairy-tale-like castle that rose higher than the surrounding mounds of snow. Through the frost-laced windows of this wondrous Gothic structure I glimpsed chandeliers blazing with light. We were approaching the imposing Victoria Hall.

"Did we make it, Daddy?" Anxiously, I broke our three-hour silence. "Are we going to be on time?"

Daddy raised the sleeve of his jacket and checked the face of his wristwatch. A barely perceptible sigh escaped his lips and was caught by particles of frigid air.

I would make it to the dressing room before the two o'clock matinee. So would every other child scheduled to appear on stage that afternoon. The silver metal band of Daddy's wristwatch glittered in glints of cold winter sun... "Noela!

Look!" Breaking into my reverie, Dark Honey indicated the view. "Look how far you've come!" We had reached a clearing on a summit. What confronted us was a spectacular vista of sugar-frosted cedars and pine.

"Man, you're tough-minded." Dark Honey's cheeks glowed with the cold.

"Who, me?" My lungs felt close to bursting.

"Do you see anyone else around?" Only I could perceive Daddy's spirit as it receded into the ether. "You pushed past your exhaustion. You made it." In homage, Dark Honey bowed. "You showed the mountain who's boss!"

On a summit, in a clearing, I paused to catch my breath. The greater the distance, the clearer the view.

ABOUT THE AUTHOR

S. Nadja Zajdman is a Canadian author. Her fiction and non-fiction writing has been featured in newspapers, magazines, literary journals and anthologies across North America, in the UK, Australia and New Zealand. In 2021 Zajdman received an award from The Society of Authors Foundation in London.

Hobart Books (Oxford) has published *I Want You To Be Free*, a memoir of her late mother, the trailblazing Holocaust educator and activist Renata Skotnicka-Zajdman. In 2011, terminally ill, Skotnicka-Zajdman was awarded the Polish government's Order of Merit.

Following the publication of this linked story collection *The Memory Keeper,* Bridge House will be bringing out a second story collection, *Bent Branches*.

Recently Nadja Zajdman completed work on a comic novel of love and desire at a seniors' centre.

LIKE TO READ MORE WORK LIKE THIS?

Then sign up to our mailing list and download our free collection of short stories, *Magnetism*. Sign up now to receive this free e-book and also to find out about all of our new publications and offers.

Sign up here:
   http://eepurl.com/gbpdVz

PLEASE LEAVE A REVIEW

Reviews are so important to writers. Please take the time to review this book. A couple of lines is fine.

Reviews help the book to become more visible to buyers. Retailers will promote books with multiple reviews.

This in turn helps us to sell more books… And then we can afford to publish more books like this one.

Leaving a review is very easy.

Go to https://smarturl.it/gy9vdq, scroll down the left-hand side of the Amazon page and click on the "Write a customer review" button.

OTHER WRITING BY S. NADJA ZAJDMAN

I Want You To Be Free
Published by Hobart Books

Told by her daughter, the Canadian author S. Nadja Zajdman, this is the true story of one woman's escape from hell in the Warsaw Ghetto to her eventual migration to a new life in Montreal.

Born in 1928 to a privileged but troubled Jewish family, Renata Skotnicka-Zajdman's upbringing was rich in culture and secular appreciation of the society around her, factors that would one day save her life.

After surviving the initial siege of Warsaw, from 1939 Renata endured over two years of life on the run before being incarcerated in Warsaw's infamous Ghetto. She was one of the few children to survive its conditions, thanks to the watchful guidance of her older brother and sister, as well as the heroism of eight Catholic rescuers.

Paperback: ISBN 978-1-914322-09-9

Available from Hobart Books at
www.hobartbooks.com/product-page/i-want-you-to-be-free

Short Stories

A Wedding in Heidelberg
Published by The Saturday Evening Post
February 2015

In this historical fiction by S. Nadja Zajdman, relief workers, soldiers, and refugees gather for a Jewish wedding in the American-occupied zone of post-war Germany.

www.saturdayeveningpost.com/2015/02/wedding-heidelberg

Intensive Care
Published by Storyhouse
March 2020

A portrait of Dr Jean Liard, Born January 1926, died November 10, 1981. Worthy of Memory

www.storyhouse.org/snadja4.html

OTHER PUBLICATIONS BY BRIDGE HOUSE

The House on Schellberg Street

by Gill James

Renate Edler loves to visit her grandmother in the house on Schellberg Street. She often meets up with her friend Hani Gödde who lives nearby. This year, though, it is not to be. Just a few weeks after a night when synagogues are burned and businesses owned by Jews are looted, Renate finds out a terrible secret about her family.

At a time when the world is at war and the horrors of the Holocaust are slowly becoming apparent, Renate has to leave behind her home and her friends, and become somebody she never thought she could be.

The house on Schellberg Street needs to stay strong. Will it and those who work in it be strong enough? Will Renate ever feel at home again? And what of those left behind?

"A must-read for anyone studying World war II. Anyone who enjoyed *The Boy with the Striped Pyjamas* will love it." *(Amazon)*

Order from Amazon:
ISBN: 978-1-910542-23-1 (paperback)
978-1-910542-24-8 (ebook)

Chapeltown Books

Clara's Story: a Holocaust Biography

by Gill James

Clara will not be daunted. Her life will not end when her beloved husband dies too young. She will become a second mother to the young children who live away from home at a rather special school – a particular class of disabled children growing up in Nazi Germany.

Clara's Story: a Holocaust Biography is the second story in the Schellberg Cycle. It might be described as a tragedy or it might be described as a story of survival. In the end it is up to the reader or even Clara herself to decide.

"The social history starting before World War 1, and continuing to the present day, was extremely interesting and Clara herself had the attitude that where there's hope there's life. A well-written and thought-provoking book." *(Amazon)*

Order from Amazon:
ISBN: 978-1-910542-33-0 (paperback)
978-1-910542-34-7 (ebook)

Chapeltown Books

Girl in a Smart Uniform

by Gill James

Girl in a Smart Uniform is the third book in the Schellberg Cycle, a collection of novels inspired by a bundle of photocopied letters that arrived at a small cottage in Wales in 1979. The letters give us first-hand insights into what life was like growing up in Germany in the 1930s and 1940s.

It is the most fictional of the stories to date, though some characters, familiar to those who have read the first two books, appear again here. Clara Lehrs, Karl Schubert and Dr Kühn really existed. We have a few, a very few, verifiable facts about them. The rest we have had to find out by repeating some of their experiences and by using the careful writer's imagination.

Girl in a Smart Uniform
Gill James

"The book is well written and easy to read. The girl's home life is complicated and there are some moving develop-ments involving her brothers. Thoroughly worth reading!" *(Amazon)*

Order from Amazon:
ISBN: 978-1-910542-10-1 (paperback)
978-1-910542-11-8 (ebook)

Chapeltown Books